saHaLee Inn

A Dora and Dick Carlson Mystery

T.P. Wintermute

Prismatist Press

Book Cover Art by Don Nisbett and Book Cover Design by Kiley Grantges

ISBN 979-8-9894234-1-5

eISBN 979-8-9894234-0-8

For Kathleen

Contents

CHAPTER ONE

"We've got bats," Dick announced as he walked toward his wife who was on her knees pruning one of the flower beds near the entrance to the Sahalee Inn.

"Where?" Dora asked as she got to her feet.

"In the belfry. I decided to check out the view from the top of the steeple. When I reached the belfry, after taking those winding stairs, which leads to a dizzying height, I must say, I discovered that we not only have bells hanging up there, but bats as well."

"How did that happen?" Dora demanded, waving the pruning shears.

"How? This was a church before it was an inn for God's sake, so of course it has a steeple and steeples have belfries and belfries have bats, that's how."

"Of course, dear, I know this was originally a church. After all, our new brochure and website explain that the church was built on this hill overlooking Ilwaco harbor because it's called Sahalee and Sahalee means high heavenly place in the Chinook language. Then when Farley McTavish converted the church into an inn he decided to call it Sahalee Inn with the motto, *A heavenly place to stay.*"

"Okay," Dick replied, without admitting that he hadn't read the new brochure or given the website anything but a rudimentary glance. "Since this is a heavenly place, maybe they're not bats in the belfry but angels. In that case, it would probably be bad luck or karma or something to exterminate them."

"Exterminate! We don't want them harmed in any way. Bats serve an important role in the environment like pollinating flowers."

"We could see if any bat caves around here have a vacancy."

"Now you're just being silly instead of a supportive spouse. Remember that we agreed when we got married that I would help you in your career as a detective…"

"A criminologist, Dora. I have a PhD, remember."

"Oh, Dr. Dick, how could I forget, since I typed your thesis." Dora tucked the shears under her left elbow and pantomimed typing. "My point is that we had an agreement that I would fully support you as you pursued your career as a criminologist. You never heard a peep from me, even when you were off gallivanting all over the world."

"Gallivanting? Is that how you characterize my work as a consulting criminologist?"

"No, of course not, dear. I'm proud that you helped nab all those bad people. In fact, that's why you shouldn't have any trouble with those bats in our belfry."

"But from what you just told me bats aren't bad, they're good, and criminologists don't catch good people, much less good bats. Maybe I should just ring the bells. That should scare them away."

"And traumatize them? No way."

"Yes, I suppose we don't want bats flying around with post-traumatic stress disorder."

Dora threw up her arms. "Now I've forgotten what we were talking about to begin with."

"Something about me gallivanting around the world."

"Oh, yes. You agreed that after we were married twenty-five years, you would retire, and it would be my turn to pursue a career of my own. Five years ago, I told you my dream was to be an innkeeper and that I wanted to buy an inn near the water and I've been planning it ever since."

"Okay, but I didn't think we'd be relocating across the country from New York to the West Coast."

"Not the West Coast, Dick, specifically the Pacific Northwest Coast. There's a big difference between here and Hollywood."

"I just thought that when you said you wanted to buy an inn overlooking the water it would be a three-bedroom unit in our building on the Upper West Side, only half a block from Riverside Drive that you'd turn it into a B & B. When I say B & B, I'm referring to a bed and breakfast, not bats and belfry."

"Seriously, Dick, there's no comparison between looking at New Jersey across the polluted Hudson River and this view of the picturesque Ilwaco harbor with fishing boats heading out into the Columbia River toward the Pacific just beyond Cape Disappointment."

Cape Disappointment, the rocky headland in the distance, described Dick's feelings when Dora had announced that she wanted to buy the Sahalee Inn, but he wisely kept it to himself. Instead, he took the white handkerchief he always kept in his pants pocket, pressed and unsoiled in case he needed to pick up a piece of evidence, and waved it in surrender. "Okay, okay, dear. Besides the deed is done. In fact, it's signed, sealed, and recorded. We're now the owners."

"Innkeepers, honey. Actually, I'm the innkeeper and you're the innkeeper's spouse."

"Not even Assistant Innkeeper, huh?"

"Martin's the Assistant Innkeeper."

"I thought he was the desk clerk."

"That's just one of his duties. Besides you'd never agree to be an assistant to anyone."

"True." Dick nodded his head. "What are my duties as the innkeeper's spouse?"

"To be supportive of his spouse like she was supportive of him for twenty-five years. Oh, and also be nice and schmooze with the guests, but not about scary serial killers or that sort of thing."

"No shamus schmoozing," Dick shrugged. "So what do I talk about?"

"About the area. Its history, flora, and fauna, where to hike and fish, that sort of thing."

"I don't know anything about this area." Unlike Dora, who'd been there for six weeks to oversee the transition of Sahalee Inn from the old owner, Dick had stayed behind in New York to arrange for the sale of their condo. "I suppose I know something about hiking from walking in Manhattan. They say that New Yorkers are the fastest walkers in the world."

"That's because they're always in a rush to get someplace or to get away from someone," Dora said. "Here people hike to be in the beautiful surroundings that nature provides."

Sounds like a Sunday stroll in Central Park, Dick was about to say, but, as a supportive spouse, thought that he should keep his mouth shut.

"Just do some research," Dora continued. "You know all about how to do research. After all, as you pointed out, you have a PhD. Just change your research focus from crime to some interesting things about the area that would entertain our guests."

"I prefer enlighten."

"Then enlighten them about the area with an emphasis on light."

"I doubt that there are any dark deeds around here to talk about," Dick replied, hiding his disappointment.

"Other than that, just be supportive, dear. I'll run the inn along with the help of the staff."

"You mean Martin the desk clerk and Elspeth the maid."

"I told you, Martin is the Assistant Innkeeper and Elspeth is the Housekeeper. They've both worked here for years. The only employee I've had to hire is Lars."

"Who's Lars?"

"Lars is the new handyman."

"What happened to the old handyman?"

"He was more old than handy..."

"We're no spring chickens ourselves," Dick interrupted.

"Speak for yourself, dear," Dora replied in mock rebuke. "I feel young all over again. Anyway, you didn't let me finish. What I meant was that when I met him it was clear that the experience one assumes comes with age had somehow eluded him. Anyway, he announced when I met him that he was quitting so that he could devote himself to fishing full-time. According to Martin that was what he already was doing. It was Martin who recommended Lars."

"I assume he's qualified."

"He worked in the hardware store his family owns, so he should know all about tools and things."

"Knowing about something doesn't necessarily mean you know how to do anything."

"That's what they say about PhDs, isn't it, that they live in an ivory tower?" Dora teased. "Speaking of ivory towers brings us back to what to do about the bats that live in the belfry. I'll have Lars remove them. Humanely of course."

"So there's nothing you need me for other than to be sociably enlightening?"

"You can display both at our happy hour when we welcome our guests. It isn't until four, so if you have some time to do a little research before then it would help. It's eleven now so you have five hours."

"It would help me with my research if I knew what our guests might be interested in."

"Why don't you ask Martin?" Dora said, clicking the blades of the shears together several times for emphasis. "And take Watson with you. He needs the exercise."

Dick looked at the bloodhound sleeping on the grass. "Come on Watson, get off your haunches. The game's afoot."

Martin was standing behind the front desk. He seemed to Dick to be the result of crossbreeding an English butler with a Norwegian bachelor farmer.

"I wonder if you can help me with some research, Martin?"

"Research, Mr. Carlson, or should I call you Dr.?"

"I'm not a medical doctor. My doctorate is in criminology."

"Criminology?"

"Unlike a medical doctor who only needs to know medicine, a Doctor of Criminology has to know sociology, psychology, psychiatry, biology, social anthropology, and philosophy."

"Philosophy as well," Martin nodded sagely. "It must keep you busy."

"It does. I mean it did. But now that we bought this place, my criminology days are behind me. I suppose there isn't much crime around here, anyway?"

"Oh, I don't know about that, Mr., I mean Dr. ..."

"Just call me Dick."

"Of course, I'm not an expert on crime any more than I am on medicine, Dick, but if you want to research crime around here – not that there's a problem, mind you – you can read about it right here in the Cape Disappointment Dispatch. They print the local police and sheriff reports and jail bookings every week. It's probably the most popular part of the paper."

"Really? Can you read me one of the reports?"

"Let's see," Martin flipped the pages, stopped and hunched over. "On Wednesday suspicious activity was reported at the Sleepy Salmon Motel at 12:19 a.m."

"I guess it wasn't the salmon who called the police since he would have been asleep."

"They don't print the names of the callers."

"Just joking, Martin. Does it say what the suspicious activity was?"

Martin looked at the paper and shook his head, "It doesn't. This is just what people call in to the police. I can tell you, though, there's a lot of suspicious activity at the Sleepy Salmon. Unlike here."

"Can I borrow that?"

"Borrow it? You can have it. There's a stack here," Martin tapped the pile lying beside him on the desk. "We give them to our guests when they check in. It gives them a sense as to what goes on around here."

"Including the suspicious activities."

"Oh, you're just joking again, aren't you, Dick?"

"In any case, I'm not here to research suspicious activity, but rather of the less suspicious variety. The kind of activities that might be of interest to our guests, as opposed to those who stay at the Sleepy Salmon."

"Oh, we have lots of activities of that nature around here. For example, there's fishing. Our guests can charter a fishing boat at the port and fish in the river or the ocean, if they don't mind the Bar. It can be a bit rough."

"Seems like the clientele of the Sleepy Salmon would be more into going to rough bars than our guests."

"Not that kind of bar," Martin laughed. "It's what we call the spot where the Columbia River runs into the Pacific, which I wouldn't advise for anyone prone to seasickness. The charter operators are all listed in the brochure."

"You don't recommend a specific one?"

"I don't fish. Now, Bert, he was our old handyman ..."

"Before Lars."

"Yes. Anyway, if a guest had a question about fishing I'd ask Bert to speak with them. The only problem was that Bert could go on and on."

"And now he's gone ... fishing, from what I understand."

"Yes, old Bert is fishing full-time. Has his own boat and takes people out. Gives our guests a ten percent discount."

"And if they get seasick, he gives them a pail to puke in," Dick said half-seriously.

"No need for a pail," Martin replied in all seriousness. "They can puke right over the side of the boat."

"What other things are there that would interest our guests?" Dick asked.

"Since this is the Long Beach Peninsula, and we have the longest beach in the world, that's at the top of the list."

"Really? The longest beach? Who made that determination?"

Martin scratched his chin, then said, "I don't know exactly, but that's what everyone's always said. In fact, it's right here in this brochure the Visitors' Bureau puts out." Martin picked up a brochure. "We have a bunch of them in this rack here. There are a lot of other brochures as well, so if you take one of each ..."

"I don't want the guests to think that they could just read these brochures and know as much as I do."

Martin put the brochure down. "You know a lot more about research than I do, Dick. You just ask your questions and I'll do my best."

"Thanks Martin. So, getting back to the beach. If it's the longest beach in the world it must have plenty of activities."

"Well, you can ride horses on the beach, you can ride bikes on the beach, and go clam digging in season. And, of course, you can fly a kite. The wind is very good for kite-flying. We have an international kite-flying contest every year."

"I like the idea of telling someone to go fly a kite as something other than an insult," Dick smiled. "What about swimming in the ocean?"

Martin shook his head. "Not advisable, I'm afraid."

"Too cold?"

"That and the currents are very treacherous. They can pull you way out and under before you know it."

"Yes, I could see that we should discourage that. It could lead to an early checkout for our guests. What about wading?"

"Oh, yes, you can wade but you should avoid turning your back to the ocean. There are rogue waves that can come up from behind and before you know it ..."

"I get it, you're waving 'bye-bye' for good. I assume it's okay to sit on the beach and look at the ocean? Maybe take a nap?"

"Certainly. Just don't fall asleep when the tide is coming in and make sure that you're visible so that you don't get run over."

"I guess that means that if any of our guests want to go for a jog on the beach, they should be careful not to run over our guests who are sunbathing."

"Good point, although I was referring to being run over by moving vehicles. You see, the beach is also considered a highway by the State of Washington."

"So, another activity for our guests is to drive on the beach."

"But they shouldn't speed or they can get a ticket. It's also easy to get stuck in the sand, which is not a good predicament if the tide is coming in."

"In other words our guests should watch out for speed bumps that might be sunbathers, sand traps and speed traps. What about the other side of the peninsula?"

"There's no beach on the east, Willapa Bay, side, just oyster beds."

"No rogue waves to worry about, although I suppose you have to watch out for bad oysters. But from what you've told me, Martin, I can see that there's a lot to do. Since I don't have much time, it would help me in my research if you could tell me something about our guests."

"I'm afraid I can't provide you with much background on our guests."

"Surely you have something on the computer?" Dick patted the screen on the desktop.

Martin punched the keys and then turned the screen around so that Dick could look at it. "You can have a gander, but as you see all that's required to book a room is the guest's name, address, the type of room they want, and a credit card."

"What about this?" Dick jabbed his right index finger at a spot on the screen. "It asks if they are bringing any children or pets."

"That's for the extra damage deposit we charge for the pets."

"Quite right. Pets can wreak havoc." Watson barked and Dick looked down at him. "I wasn't talking about you, Watson. You're not a pet, but rather a colleague." Turning back to Martin, Dick asked. "Why don't we charge a damage deposit for children?"

"That wouldn't be very family-friendly. We just want to make sure that what they've booked is appropriate. You would be surprised how a couple will show up with three or four children in tow, and all they've reserved is one room with a double bed. Now, as you can see, two of our guests are bringing one child with them. Actually, they're not children but teenagers, and no one is bringing any pets."

"And that's the only information we have on them?"

"We also require a credit card or a cash deposit."

"I have to say, Martin, I'm a bit disappointed that this is the only background information we collect."

"I believe collecting that kind of information would violate our Sahalee Inn code of ethics that pledges we respect the privacy of our guests. It's posted right here on the wall." Martin pointed to a framed document on the wall next to the desk.

Dick looked at the document, then said, "It might need to be updated. Times change."

"It was your wife who gave it to me this morning and said she wanted it displayed prominently near the front desk."

On the other hand, some things never change, Dick thought. "Maybe you can just run off the information that you have so I can at least know their names and where they're from."

Martin printed out the list and handed it to Dick. "These are for the rooms that have been reserved. We have one still vacant and we're likely to get some walk-ins."

Dick scanned the list as he started to walk away. He stopped and came back to the desk and asked Martin. "It says here that some of our rooms have been reserved by the Eidolonic Society. That's an unusual name."

"The man who made the reservation didn't say what it meant. He only mentioned that it was a field trip."

"Hmmm. And what is this Campanology Club next to this woman's name? Sounds like a club for companies."

"Oh no, Dick," Martin chuckled. "It's a fancy name for our local bellringers club. They've been meeting here every Sunday for more than fifty years, going back to when this was still a church."

"They meet to talk about bellringing?"

"I suppose they do before and afterwards. It would be pretty difficult to hear themselves talk while they're ringing the bells."

"Ringing the bells ... in our belfry?"

"Where else would the bells be?"

"Doesn't it disturb the guests?"

"Quite the contrary. What would a Sunday be without church bells?"

"This isn't a church anymore."

"None of the churches that are still used as churches have bells, so these are the only church bells to be heard," Martin responded. "In any case, we've never had any complaints. Besides, most of our guests check out Sunday morning and new guests don't check in until four. They can only ring the bells from two to four. It's all part of the agreement with the city."

"What do you mean 'agreement with the city'?"

"Oh, I see you don't know about the agreement? Well then, I suppose I should explain. You see when the church was converted to an inn the city said that it not only had to keep the steeple, which is quite a landmark, you must admit, but that the bells couldn't be removed and they had to be rung at least once a week. The Campanology Club had insisted that the city require it. Mrs. Carlson knows all about the bell ringing."

"She might know about the bells, but she didn't know about the bats in the belfry."

"They're such a fixture that I didn't even think of mentioning them to her."

"Well, they're fixing to go because Dora is going to have Lars remove them. Humanely, of course."

CHAPTER TWO

Maybe it was the Columbia River on the other side of the breakwater, maybe the Pacific Ocean in the distance, maybe the water lapping against the boats bobbing in the harbor, or maybe it was seeing the name In the Drink Pub on the sign, but the most probable cause as to why Dick and Watson were thirsty was the six blocks they'd walked in bright sunlight from the Sahalee Inn to Ilwaco Harbor.

They had then strolled along the paved promenade between the harbor and an eclectic mix of businesses, including art galleries, fresh fish shops, charter boat operations, and, Dick noted with particular interest, a bookstore with a bakery-café next door. At the end of the promenade, just beyond the pub, was a pier with a large red building and 'Bessie's Best Seafood' painted on it in bold black letters.

Dick sat down at one of the pub's outside picnic tables. After ordering a pint of Cape D Dark Ale and a bowl of water for

Watson from a waiter wearing a *Drown your Sorrows at In the Drink Pub* t-shirt, he took in the harbor scene. Other than the Staten Island Ferry, Dick had hardly been on a boat, and he'd never been on a large trawler like those moored in the harbor alongside the smaller fishing boats and pleasure crafts. He was one of the rare readers who had actually finished Herman Melville's *Moby Dick*, but only because he wanted to find out why the great white whale was named Dick. Although he was disappointed that he never learned the origin of the name, he acquired an encyclopedic knowledge on the subject of whales and the whaling industry. Dick wondered if any of it would be useful if he went out on one of these fishing boats. Maybe there was a Great White Tuna with his name on it lurking in the ocean beyond Cape Disappointment?

A woman's voice interrupted Dick's nautical thoughts. "Mind if I sit down?"

Dick looked up and saw an attractive woman in jeans. "Not at all," he replied. Seeing the gold badge pinned to the left breast pocket of her blue shirt he added, "You must be with the local Police Department?"

She pulled on her badge and looked at it. "You're right, that's what it says."

Dick leaned toward her. "It also says Chief of Police."

"It's probably there to remind me."

Dick held out his right hand. "Well, Chief, good to meet you."

"Sally Gilmore," she answered, shaking his hand. "Everyone calls me Sally instead of Chief. Everyone except the people I've arrested, and I won't repeat the things they call me."

"Dick Carlson," Dick said.

Sally nodded. "You're Dora's husband."

"You know who I am?"

"The only thing that travels fast around here is the local news and gossip, and most of the time it's hard to tell the difference," Sally laughed. "Anyway, as soon as I heard that there was a new owner of the inn, I went over and introduced myself right away. Dora told me that you were a criminologist before you retired."

"I still dabble in it."

Sally laughed, "Most of the crimes committed around here are by dabblers."

"I know, I read the police report in the local paper. Don't you get bored?"

"After twenty years with the Seattle Police boring is fine with me."

"How long have you been here?"

"Several years, although I've been coming here since I was a kid. My family has long had a summer house farther up the peninsula in Ocean Park. I always wanted to retire here, so when the Chief of Police position came up, I figured it was the next best thing. As it turns out, it's the best thing." She was interrupted by the waiter handing her a mug of coffee. "For a bar, they make pretty good coffee here," Sally said, taking a sip.

"Of course, it's even better with a shot of whiskey in it, but I'm on duty."

After taking a swig from the pint glass, Dick said, "The beer isn't bad and I don't think it would be better in coffee." Then, turning to Watson, who was sitting on his haunches next to what was now a half-empty bowl of water, he added, "Watson seems to like the water as well."

Sally stood up and looked over the top of the picnic table at Watson. "A bloodhound. An apt pet for a criminologist," she said.

Watson opened an eye and looked at Sally then closed it again. Dick patted Watson on his head. "Watson isn't just a pet, he's my partner in crime... solving. He's downright dogged in his pursuit once he's gotten hold of a criminal's scent."

"He doesn't appear to be sniffing anything at the moment," Sally said as she sat down. "So, I guess I'll be able to finish my coffee." She started to take a sip when suddenly Watson jumped up and barked. A skateboard ridden by a man with a scraggly beard and long stringy hair shot by, hotly pursued by a boy in his early teens screaming, "Thief!"

"Or maybe not," Sally said as she jumped up then started running after them.

Dick got up, unleashed Watson, and said, "The game's afoot, Watson."

Immediately, Watson leaped forward like a racehorse out of the starting gate. Although most people think that bloodhounds move slowly with their nose to the ground, they can also run up to thirty miles an hour, and in no time at all he had overtaken Sally, passed the kid, and was alongside the skateboarder, barking loudly all the way. The skateboarder shook one of his feet at Watson who responded by sinking his teeth into the back of the skateboard, pulling it from under the man's feet. The man continued on without the board, running down the grassy bank between the promenade and the harbor and into the water.

By the time Dick arrived on the scene, Watson was sitting on his haunches with the skateboard in front of him, being petted by the boy. The man was flailing in the water between the shore and a floating dock shouting that he didn't know how to swim. Sally calmly walked onto the gangway that connected the shore to the dock, detached a life ring from a stanchion and threw it at the man, who quickly grabbed it. She pulled him over to a ladder by the rope attached to the preserver and onto the dock as if she were reeling in a fish. From his vantage point on the promenade, Dick was unable to hear Sally question the man, but when she slapped on a pair of handcuffs it was clear that she wasn't happy with his answers. He couldn't help noticing that the name of the boat moored next to them was *Nauti Buoy*. A minute later she led the soaked man back onto the promenade.

Dick and Watson accompanied Sally as she escorted her prisoner to her patrol car in the parking lot. After locking the man in the back seat, she told Dick that there had been a rash of skateboard thefts. "The ones stolen were top of the line and worth $150-$200 new, even more. They're easy to re-sell on e-commerce sites. Tommy – he's the victim – said the one the guy was trying to steal is a Sector 9 Monkey King that he just got for his birthday. He's from Portland and is here with his family on vacation. They're renting a house a couple of blocks away and he skateboarded over here to get a smoothie at The Snack Attack. As he was ordering, the suspect snatched the board and took off. I called his parents and they're coming to pick him up. They'll bring him over to the station so we can get his statement." Sally bent down and petted Watson. "Thanks to your help, Watson, we caught our skateboard thief red-handed, or maybe red-footed is more appropriate."

Watson barked as the patrol car pulled away. Dick looked down at Watson and said, "I know what you're thinking, if this were New York, it would have been more of a challenge to catch a skateboard thief, but at least you got some exercise in the fresh air." Dick and Watson walked back to the pub where he paid the bill. "Good thing I remembered to pay or we'd end up on the Ilwaco Most Wanted list," he explained to Watson. Looking at his watch Dick saw that he still had some time before he needed to be back at the inn, so he walked over to Ballast Books and tied Watson's leash to a bicycle rack outside. When he entered, a middle-aged woman sitting behind the counter cheerfully asked if she could help him.

Overcoming his native New Yorker suspicion of friendly salesclerks, Dick put on a smile and replied, "I'm new here and was wondering what books you have on the area."

"They're in our Local Interest section right next to you. Most of the authors are from this area."

Dick started looking at the titles, pulled one out, and read aloud, *Unsolved Mysteries of Cape Disappointment.* He looked at the table of contents then said to the woman, "I wouldn't have thought there were this many unsolved mysteries around here."

She gave a hearty laugh. "It may be due more to a deficiency when it comes to detecting than their unsolvability." She walked over and held out her hand. "My name is Tillie, by the way. I'm the owner."

Dick shook her hand. "Dick."

She looked at the bookcase. "I haven't had a chance to restock these shelves. The new owner of the Sahalee Inn came in yesterday and bought a lot of books for their library including ones from this section. She said that she hoped her guests would be interested in more than Clive Cussler and Danielle Steel. It's funny, but she also said that she didn't want to buy the book you're holding because it might tempt her husband."

"And she's right. I am tempted."

"You're her husband?"

Dick bowed then asked, "Have you read this book?"

"Sure have," Tillie answered, still red in the face. "I not only sell books, I actually read them. Each chapter describes a different mysterious occurrence. Ghosts, shipwrecks, murders, buried treasure, they're all in there. There's everything you'd want in a mystery except finding out whodunnit at the end. There's even a chapter on the inn."

"Really? What's our unsolved mystery?"

"I wouldn't want to spoil it for you. You need to read it for yourself."

"I guess I'll have to give into temptation and buy the book then." Dick pulled out his wallet and handed Tillie a credit card. "Does this Morgan Murray live around here?" Dick asked, looking at the cover and reading the author's name.

"Sure does," Tillie said as she took Dick's credit card and the book. "He's quite a character, and this is a very competitive environment when it comes to characters."

"What makes him such a character?" Dick asked, following Tillie over to the counter.

"I should let you judge for yourself," she said as she ran the card.

"Where would I find him?"

Tillie handed Dick back his credit card and receipt. "He's a floater."

"You mean he floats around to different places?"

"No, I'd say he floats pretty much in one place. Morgan lives on his boat in the harbor. Although he claims to use the boat for charter fishing, it hardly slips its moorings. You can probably find him there right now." She handed Dick the book. "I'm sure he'd love to autograph your copy of his book."

Dick looked at his watch. "Maybe later. I should be getting back to the inn. Where can I find his boat?"

"It's hard to fathom."

"I'm sure I can figure it out if you give me the name."

"*Hard to Fathom* is the name of the boat. Fathom is the unit for measuring the depth of water. It's equal to six feet."

"That's the same depth that bodies are usually buried," Dick noted.

"Six feet under," Tillie chuckled. "Why, I never thought of it that way. Of course, that's six feet under the earth in a cemetery. Who knows how many fathoms under are the bodies buried out there in the water of what's called 'the Graveyard of the Pacific.'"

After leaving the Ballast with book in hand, Dick decided that a coffee would be nice to drink as he strolled back to the inn. He opted not to wake Watson who was snoring contentedly and entered the Grist and Grind, the bakery-café next door. The place was empty except for one of the three booths that flanked the large picture window. Dick walked toward the counter where a young woman behind the counter was leaning on her elbows and looking at her cellphone. Alerted by the ringing of the bell over the door when he entered, she pocketed the phone and was flashing a smiling face by the time he got to the counter.

"I'd like a large coffee to go," Dick said.

"Would you like one of our espresso drinks?" She nodded at the machine next to her. "Lattes, cappuccinos, americanos ..."

"Just a plain old coffee."

"We don't sell old coffee, it's all fresh." She sounded hurt.

"I didn't mean old that way, I meant not one of those espresso drinks." Dick apologized.

Her glossy red lips relaxed back into a smile and asked. "Hot or iced coffee?"

"Hot."

"Do you want it with fresh cream, half and half, whole milk, two percent, nonfat, almond or oat milk?"

"None of the above."

"One hot, black coffee," she confirmed. "Can I tempt you with one of our great, fresh-baked homemade pastries? You won't find anything better in town."

"Is there another bakery in town?"

"Well, no." Her smile evaporated and quickly reappeared. "But even if there were, we would still be the best."

Deciding that it was best to surrender, Dick bent down and looked at the pastries on display behind the glass front of the counter. "Okay, I'll take a brownie."

She perked up. "Which kind? We have peanut butter, walnut, fudge, and our special of the day, cranberry. Wait, I forgot that I just sold our last cranberry brownie. Sorry."

"Would you happen to have just a nothing special, regular old...I mean fresh, chocolate brownie?"

"I think so," she answered. After searching around in the display case, she removed one of the brownies from a tray and dropped it into a white paper bag. As she picked up a paper to-go cup and turned to fill it from the coffee urn behind her she asked, "How long will you be staying?"

"I'm not. That's why I asked for takeout."

"I mean how long are you visiting Ilwaco?"

"Why do you think I'm just visiting?"

"I grew up here and can pretty much tell who's a local and who's not."

"Well, I was a not, but I just moved here so now I guess I just am. My name is Dick Carlson, by the way."

"I'm Nicole." After they shook hands, she asked, "Where did you move from?"

"New York City."

The girl turned and looked at him, her blue eyes wide open in amazement. "No way!"

"Trust me there is a way, because I'm here."

She knitted her brows, one of which Dick now noticed was pierced by a silver ring. "I'm just surprised that someone would actually move ... here ... all the way ... from New York City."

"You and me both. It was my wife Dora's idea. Her dream, actually."

"Her dream was to live here?" she asked in astonishment, fastening a lid on the to-go cup and handing it to Dick.

"Her dream was to own an inn and it turned out that the inn we bought happens to be here."

"Oh my god!" she exclaimed. "You must be the new owners of the Sahalee Inn."

"I guess we must be."

"I can't wait to see what you do with the place. Are you thinking of reopening the restaurant?"

"That's up to my wife, Dora. As I said, the inn is her dream."

Nicole rested her elbows on the counter, looked at him dreamily and said, "It's so romantic."

"You think the inn is a good place for romantic getaways?"

"I mean it's so romantic that you were willing to leave New York City and come all the way across the country so that your wife's dream could come true. I wish my boyfriend would be willing to make my dream come true, but he's afraid."

Dick nodded his head, "You wish he'd propose, but your boyfriend's afraid of making a commitment, huh?"

Nicole snapped out of her dream state and looked at Dick. "Propose? I don't want to get married. My wish is that Zeke would ask his father to lend us the money so we can open a restaurant, but he's afraid to." She handed Dick the white bag. "Anyway, here's your plain brownie to go. I bet you're taking it back for your wife, right?"

"Of course," Dick said, tucking the *Unsolved Mysteries* book into his pants behind the small of his back and grabbing the bag. "I am now."

CHAPTER THREE

Dick stood next to the small bar in the parlor off the Sahalee Inn's lobby. Although he was decked out in a blue blazer, gray slacks and a crisp white shirt, at Dora's urging to loosen up, he had forsaken a tie. Since he knew that parlor comes from the French word parler, which means "to speak," Dick felt at home in the room. The furniture consisted of wing chairs, couches and even a love seat. All were upholstered in plaids that made it look as if the furniture was engaged in the Highland Fling. Next to the bar was a device on a stand with a dial on the side and a brass lever that looked like something from a ship's bridge. Martin, who was tending the bar, explained that it was an engine order telegraph. It was salvaged from the bridge of a steam ship that ran aground on Peacock Spit off Cape Disappointment in 1905.

"The previous owner, Farley MacTavish, found it in an antique store and installed it here," Martin said, patting the lever.

"He had it rigged so you could signal the kitchen. His idea was that guests could order dinner from a menu with the telegraph's dial printed on it while they were having their drinks. An entree might have *Full Ahead* next to it and an appetizer *Half Ahead*." Martin pointed to the labels on the telegraph's dial. "The guest would then pull the handle that directed the pointer on the dial to what they wanted to order. That would ring a bell in the kitchen that signaled the cook what they wanted."

"Feed the bellies instead of the ship's boilers, huh?"

Martin sighed. "Mr. MacTavish thought it would be more efficient and save money since they wouldn't have to pay an employee to take the orders. It turned out to be much too complicated. People would pull the handle until the pointer stopped at *Full Ahead* when they should have stopped it at *Slow Ahead*, that sort of thing. It caused chaos in the kitchen, needless to say. Mrs. Teal, the cook, was ready to quit."

"So they deep-sixed it," Dick chortled.

"Yes, they switched back to having the guests order from the person tending bar who then rang up the cook on the house phone to deliver the order."

"The bartender was at the helm, in other words. Seems like the wrong person to keep everyone out of the drink. Speaking of which, I wonder if I could have a gin and tonic?"

"Might I suggest the local gin by Driftwood Distillery that is seasoned with a variety of local organically grown, handpicked herbs."

"As long as the herbs don't dilute the alcohol, why not," Dick replied.

Martin mixed the gin and tonic and handed it to Dick who took a tentative sip. He was pleasantly surprised and raised the glass toward Martin to signify that it met his approval. With glass in hand, Dick turned his attention to the guests beginning to arrive for happy hour. This would be his first go as dispenser of local lore, and stationing himself near the bar was a strategic move: Martin would be there to serve as backup in case he was stumped, as well as to refill his empty glass.

A tall, bald-headed man with a neatly trimmed goatee and black-framed glasses matching his black polo shirt walked up to the bar. Ignoring Dick, he asked Martin if he could have a Long Island iced tea.

"Might I suggest a Long Beach iced tea as an alternative," Martin answered, "with our locally grown cranberries and a vodka made by our local Driftwood Distillery?"

"I'm all for imbibing the local flavor, and I understand the peninsula is famous for its cranberries," the man said.

"Yes, the bogs are down the middle of the peninsula," Martin said as he mixed the drink.

"Oh, yes, we've got gobs of bogs, crammed with cranberries," Dick added, although he had no idea before that cranberries were grown there.

Taking the drink from Martin, the man turned to Dick. "I'm Cedric Thistlewaite."

"Thistlewaite," Dick repeated. "Why, you're part of the group from the Eidolonic Society."

"How did you know that?"

"It was on the booking form next to your name," Dick answered.

"You work here?"

"I'm the innkeeper's husband."

"So, you don't work, but your wife does."

"Every marriage requires a bit of work," Dick replied, then added. "Spouses need to support each other."

"I wouldn't know since I'm a bachelor. My work for the Eidolonic Society takes all my time and energy."

"You sound quite passionate about this Eidolonic Society."

"You could say it's the love of my life. I founded it twenty-five years ago and we've been together ever since."

"Interesting name, Eidolonic," Dick said. The name Eidolonic made Dick think of Gyrotonic, an exercise regime that was offered at the fitness center he and Dora used to go to in New York City. The equipment had pulleys and springs that reminded Dick of a medieval torture rack. He had speculated at the time whether Gyrotonics could be used to elicit a confession while exercising.

"It comes from the Greek word, *eidolon*, which means ghost or spirit."

"Does that mean it's a society of ghost hunters?"

"I prefer investigators of paranormal phenomena. We're here on a field trip."

"Cape Disappointment is called the Graveyard of the Pacific and graveyards are breeding grounds for the paranormal," Dick said, then turned to Martin for assistance. "Lots of places to find paranormal phenomena around here, right Martin?"

"Oh yes, indeed. There's Dead Man's Cove for instance. It gets its name because so many bodies from shipwrecks wash up there. Then there's North Head Light, which is supposedly haunted by a lighthouse keeper's wife who threw herself off the cliff into the ocean. Then there's ..."

Dick interrupted. "Don't we have a brochure we can give Mr. Thistlewaite?"

"No brochure, but there is the Haunted Headland Tour. Cape Disappointment is a headland."

"I know," Cedric said sharply. "Not about this tour you just mentioned, but all the rest. We've done our research on the area." Looking over Dick's shoulder he announced. "Ah, I see that the other members of my team have arrived." Turning to Martin, he said, "We're going out to dinner at the place you recommended that used to be a train station."

"The Station Restaurant," Martin said. "I'm sure you'll enjoy it."

Cedric placed his empty glass on the bar and walked off to join a small group near the front desk.

Dick returned to sipping his drink just as a woman approached. She was middle-aged with a no-nonsense hairdo, wearing black slacks and a gray sweater with a necklace of gold bells. "You must be our guest from the Campanology Club," he said.

"That rings a bell," the woman answered. "I'm Nancy Peale, and how did you know I was that guest?"

"Dick Carlson," Dick said with a bow. "I'm the official spouse of the innkeeper and unofficial greeter so I have to know a thing or two about our guests. The Campanology Club reserved a room for a Ms. Peale and I noticed the gold bells on your necklace."

"Oh these." Nancy touched the necklace with her right forefinger. "They actually have tiny clappers that move." She jiggled the necklace producing a faint ringing sound.

After Nancy ordered a glass of pinot noir, Dick commented, "You must be a virtuoso at bellringing."

"I'm not a bellringer, I'm a campanologist, someone who studies bells and bellringing."

"Sort of like me, I'm not a criminal but a criminologist. That's someone who studies crime and criminals."

"I never would have thought that campanology and criminology had anything in common," Nancy replied with a puzzled expression that passed quickly. "We campanologists do ring bells to illustrate a point when we're giving a talk."

"Although it's frowned upon for us criminologists to illustrate our talks by committing a crime, there are some things members of my profession have said that could be considered a crime."

"I assume you aren't among the guilty."

Dick shrugged his shoulders, "only by association."

"How did a criminologist become an innkeeper?"

"As I said, my wife, Dora, is the official innkeeper. I just help her out. Right now, that's by greeting the guests such as yourself and telling them about the area. Places to eat, things to see, that sort of thing."

"So you must know about the change ringing?"

"What's that, when someone fiddles with the loose change in their pocket?"

"Oh no," Nancy laughed. "Change ringing is what the Campanology Club engages in. It's much more complicated than simply ringing a bell. I mean, even a cow can ring a bell. No, this involves a number of people ringing tuned bells in a mathematically precise sequence that are known as changes. The ringers have to work as a team, just like members of an orchestra."

"And you're an expert on this change ringing as well as just plain old bellringing," Dick said, nodding his head.

"As a professor of campanology at the Bradshaw Conservatory of Music in Portland, I teach courses on change ringing. I've also written a book called *Ringing the Right Way; Advanced Change Ringing,* so I guess that makes me an expert."

Dick nodded his head in agreement. "I can see why the Campanology Club has asked you to give a talk."

"More than a talk," Nancy replied, looking at Dick with an intensity that he could only deflect with a sip of his drink. "They've asked me to help them prepare for the upcoming Pacific Northwest Change Ringing Championship. If they win that, they will be invited to the North American Championship, and if they win that, they will be in the World Championship. It's a long shot, of course. Who knows for whom the bell tolls, as we like to say in campanology."

"I don't know if they have change ringing cheerleaders at these championships, but I'm pretty good at saying cheers," Dick raised his glass of gin and tonic.

Nancy raised her glass of pinot noir and clicked his glass, then said, "When they've learned the new sequences, we'll have a performance. It will be good preparation for the first round of the championships which begins next month in Portland. Maybe the inn can help promote it since it would be helpful to practice before an audience."

"You won't have to worry about getting an audience since you can hear the bells all over town," Martin chimed in.

"But of course, we'll do our bit for our home team," Dick added.

"What's this about a home team?" The voice came from a short, stocky man in his fifties wearing a sweatsuit that didn't appear to have ever absorbed a drop of sweat.

"Our team of bellringers," Dick answered. "They're about to embark on their quest for the championship."

"What are their odds of winning? I might want to wager something."

"I don't think people bet on bellringing," Dick said, and then looked at Nancy and added, "Actually, it's change ringing, not bellringing."

"Whatever you call it, people probably bet on it," the man grinned, and then turning to Martin said, "I'll have a beer and glass of chardonnay."

"Might I suggest an IPA from our local Long Beach Brewery?" Martin replied, holding up a bottle.

"Sure," the man answered, grabbing the bottle out of Martin's hand.

With Nancy having made her escape, Dick introduced himself to the guest.

"Norm Gamble," the man said, gripping Dick's right hand like a vice. "I'm from Seattle."

"Is this your first visit to Cape Disappointment?" Dick replied, flexing his hand to bring back the circulation after Norm finished wringing it.

"Yeah, a weekend getaway. Coming here was my bride Donna's idea. You'd think the honeymoon in Hawaii would have been enough but, no, she said we needed to get out of the house to keep the romance alive." Norm grunted and then took a slug of beer. "Anyway, she's still unpacking. Amazing how much she brings for a weekend. We drove my Land Rover so there was enough room for all her baggage. I can't wait to take it for a spin on the beach. I understand they used to race cars on it. Do they have a speed limit?"

"25 miles an hour," Martin answered, saving Dick the embarrassment of not knowing.

"That would be like coasting for me."

"Well, it is the coast," Dick pointed out.

"Coasting on the coast," Norm said with a hearty laugh. "Unfortunately I can't afford another speeding ticket, so I guess I'll have to take the lead out of my shoe." Norm glanced at the entrance to the parlor and said, "Looks like my bride has arrived. I better get over with this glass of chardonnay."

Dick watched Norm strut over and hand the chardonnay to a blond woman who looked half his age. She was wearing a dress that looked like it had been sprayed on, and even without the high heels she had on, Dick figured Donna was several inches taller than Norm.

A woman's voice interrupted Dick's thoughts, "Could we have a glass of red and white wine, please?"

"Perhaps you would prefer a glass of rosé instead of mixing the two," Martin answered.

The woman blushed. "I'm sorry, I mean one glass of red and one glass of white. The red is for my husband and the white is for me."

Martin poured a glass of sauvignon blanc and a glass of cabernet. The woman handed the red to her husband, who looked the same age as his wife. Dick introduced himself.

"I'm Martha Digby and this is my husband, Gerald. We're here for the weekend with our son."

"That's right," Dick said. "You booked two adjoining rooms." He quickly explained. "I'm the inn's greeter, so if you need any advice on things to do and see ..."

"We came for the fresh air, the ocean, nature ..."

"And to get Trevor away from his computer," Gerald added grimly.

"Typical teenage boy," Martha said. "Spends all of his time at home playing games on the computer."

"Where is he now? Taking a walk or did he borrow one of our bikes for a ride?" Dick asked.

Both of them looked into their respective glasses of wine. "He's in his room playing on his computer," Martha replied, apologetically.

"But we told him," Gerald said, sticking out his chin, "that he could only use it while we are down here for cocktails. Just one hour a day for the next two days. We're even going to confiscate it at night."

"Do you want to put it in our safe?" Martin asked.

"In our safe, that's a good one," Dick chuckled and then stopped, realizing Martin was serious. "Good suggestion, I mean."

"I don't think we'll have to resort to that," Martha replied. "He's really a wonderful boy. He doesn't give us any trouble. We just think he needs to broaden his horizons beyond his computer screen."

"And get out of his room," Gerald added.

"If you're looking for a broad horizon, nothing beats the Pacific Ocean," Dick said. "I look forward to meeting ... what's your son's name again?"

"Trevor," Martha said.

"Trevor can go kite-flying, horseback riding, fishing, ride in go-carts ..."

"What about skateboarding?" Gerald asked. "We brought his board. Trevor used to skateboard before he started spending all of his time on the computer. Are there places to skateboard around here?"

"As a matter of fact, I just saw someone skateboarding at the harbor, although he did end up in the water." Dick said, deciding it was best not to tell her where the person on the skateboard ended up after that.

"Oh dear, that sounds dangerous," Martha gasped. "I hope he wasn't hurt."

While Dick was trying to think of what to say that would allay Martha's fears, Martin said, "Trevor can skateboard on the Discovery Trail. It's paved and it goes from here to Beard's Hollow and then follows the coast for six miles. Since the beach is between the trail and the ocean, if he skates off it he would just end up in the sand, not the water."

"A soft landing, as they say," Dick added.

Martin reached over to a stack of brochures at the end of the bar and handed one to Martha. "This brochure has a map of the Discovery Trail."

"There you go," Dick said with a grin. "You two can walk or ride bikes and Trevor can use his skateboard."

After thanking them for the suggestion, the Digbys walked away with brochure and wine in hand. Dick looked at his watch. He was actually disappointed that there were only fifteen more minutes. Half a dozen guests were still in the parlor. Dick noticed a male guest wearing baggy khakis and a blue work shirt, with the sleeves rolled up to the elbows, standing in front of the bookcase built into the wall on the other side of the parlor. Since Dick had yet to look at the books in the inn's library, he walked over.

"See anything you'd like to read?" Dick said.

The man turned around. Dick thought his gray hair and beard could use a trim. "Just looking," the man answered.

"We don't have any Clive Cussler or Danielle Steel books, by the way."

"Good. I detest phony adventure and phony romance," the man answered. "I was just looking at your books on local history."

"If you're a history buff you've come to the right place because lots of historic things have happened around here and none of them are phony. For example, Lewis and Clark ended their expedition here at Cape Disappointment."

"I know," the man said. "Some people think Lewis and Clark were disappointed when they finally saw the Pacific Ocean and that's why it's called Cape Disappointment. Rather it was given that name by John Meares, Captain of the *Felice Adventurer*, in 1788. Meares was looking for the entrance to a great river that he'd heard Bruno de Heceta, the Spanish explorer, had discovered at a rocky headland. After he couldn't find it, he wrote that the river didn't exist and called the rocky headland Cape Disappointment. Four years later George Vancouver also sailed past and concluded that there was no river at Cape Disappointment. Only a couple of weeks afterwards, Captain Robert Gray discovered that, indeed, the great river did exist and named it the Columbia after his ship, the *Columbia Rediviva*."

"That's like evidence of a crime being hidden in plain sight," Dick said, shaking his head.

Ignoring Dick's quip, the man continued, "To be fair, the Columbia Bar that stretches across the mouth is treacherous, and they might well have run aground and been battered to smithereens if they'd decided to take a closer look."

"Speaking of bars, how about a drink before we close ours?"

"Don't mind if I do," the man said and followed Dick over to the bar where Martin asked him, "Are you going to have your usual, Pete?"

"Yes, a whiskey sour, Martin," the man answered.

"You two know each other?" Dick was unable to hide his surprise.

"Mr. Goudy here is a regular customer," Martin replied. "Same dates every year for the past few years."

"Nothing better than a satisfied customer," Dick said. "You must really like the area."

"It has its attractions," Pete replied with a shrug then drained his whiskey sour and put the empty glass on the bar. "Now if you'll excuse me, I have something important I need to tend to." Without waiting for a reply, he turned and walked away.

"Doesn't seem like he wanted to talk," Dick said. "There must be some things that are attractive enough to bring him back every year

"The first time he came here we got into a conversation about pirates and he seemed to know a lot about them so I've often wondered if his coming back had something to do with pirates."

"If there were pirates around here we should be telling our guests," Dick jumped in with more than a little enthusiasm. "We could add digging for buried treasure when they go to the beach to the list of activities."

Martin shrugged. "When I asked Pete if pirates might have buried treasure along this stretch of the coast he clammed up." He suddenly smiled. "Come to think of it, if our guests were to go digging holes on the beach they'd be more likely to find clams than treasure."

"Am I too late to get a drink?" A woman said.

"Not at all," Martin replied. "What would you like?"

The woman looked like she could use a drink. Next to her was a teenage girl whose hair looked as if it had been tie-dyed. Her expression made it clear she'd rather be anywhere else but with her mother or at the inn or both.

"I'd like a gin martini, very dry, and my daughter, Natalya, would like ..." She turned to the teenager.

"I'd like a large glass of vodka but I don't suppose you'll give it to me, so I'll have a Coke."

"Would you like the Coke in a glass with ice?" Martin asked.

"Unless you can give me coke as white powder I can snort."

The woman gave an embarrassed laugh, "Don't mind Natalya, she likes to make jokes. Just give her a Coca-Cola in a glass with ice."

"One very dry gin martini and a Coke on the rocks, coming right up," Martin repeated. After Martin handed them their drinks, Natalya walked away. Slumping in a wing chair, she immediately pulled out her cellphone and stared at its screen.

The woman took a swig from the martini and muttered to no one in particular, "Teenagers can drive you to drink." Then, noticing Dick, she switched her drink to her left hand and held out her right. "I'm Theresa Tarantella. Most people call me Terry although some people have called me T 'n T."

"Dick Carlson," Dick responded, shaking her hand. "I'm the greeter."

"The inn has a greeter?"

"It does at the moment. I'm also married to the innkeeper."

"A supportive spouse," Terry said with some envy in her voice, then finished her martini with a second swig and asked Martin if she could have another. "Don't worry, I'm not driving. We're just going to order pizza or something."

Her second drink in hand she turned back to Dick. "I guess I needed more than one. This is supposed to be a mother-daughter weekend getaway, but after spending four hours together on our drive down from Seattle it feels like we need to get away from each other. Fortunately, I booked separate rooms." She took a sip of the martini and asked, "Any suggestions for things I can do with Natalya?"

"There are lots of mother-daughter things you can do while you're here," Dick said, giving a stiff upper lip smile. "The beach, obviously. Twenty-eight miles of it. Great for sunbathing."

"I'd love that, but Natalya would probably find that boring. She also is into the pale look. It goes with her hair."

"Horseback riding," Martin offered. "That's something that you can do together and in a group that usually includes other teenagers."

"Yes, horseback riding. Natalya loves horses. When she was younger she begged me and Brian, that's my ex-husband, to buy her a horse. Brian said absolutely not. That we should buy her a dog and she'd forget about horses. Of course we had to buy the dog Brian wanted. It was a pit bull named Buster who terrorized half our neighborhood. Finally, I got rid of him."

"You euthanized it?" Dick asked.

"No, I divorced him and insisted as part of the settlement that Brian get custody of Buster. I got the house and he got the doghouse." She smiled at the thought and took another sip from her martini. "Anyway, the divorce was nasty, but it just became final, and I thought this would be a good way to get both of our minds off it."

"And now is your chance to rekindle your daughter's love of horses," Martin suggested sympathetically.

"I'll settle for a few hours of her not hating me," Terry said, and finished her martini. "It's certainly worth trying. I'll see if she's interested." She walked over and sat next to Natalya. Dick couldn't hear what they were saying but it seemed that it was a good sign when Natalya stopped looking at her smartphone. Finally, Terry turned to Dick and Martin and made an okay sign with her left hand.

As the grandfather clock began to chime six o'clock, signaling the end of the cocktail hour, Dick ordered another gin and tonic.

"One for the road?"

"No, one for Dora," Dick answered. "Here she comes now."

Martin quickly made the drink and handed it to Dick who handed it to Dora, just as she arrived at the bar.

"Thank you, honey," Dora said. "How did it go?"

"The drinking was swell. Martin knows his way around the bar. I'm referring to this one, not the Columbia Bar, although he probably could steer a ship over it without a scratch."

"I mean, with the guests, silly," she said jabbing Dick in the right arm.

"Careful, honey, that's my drinking arm. But to answer your question, I think I managed not to let the home team down. Of course, I couldn't have done it without Martin's coaching. I guess you can teach an old dog new tricks." Watson barked and Dick bent down, patted his head, and said, "I didn't mean you, Watson. You already know everything."

CHAPTER FOUR

Things go bang in the night, especially in a hundred-year-old inn, but when bells are ringing you can't help but sit up and notice, which is exactly what Dora did. "See what's going on," she said, giving Dick a nudge that nearly rolled him off the bed onto the hardwood floor.

"Sure, honey," Dick replied groggily, getting out of bed and putting on his slippers and bathrobe over his pajamas.

"Be careful, it could be a thief."

"If it is they've set off a hell of a burglar alarm."

"Wait, I'm going with you," Dora said. "After all the innkeeper is like the captain of a ship."

"Then you should be on the bridge, wherever that is."

"The front desk. I'll be there while you find out what this is all about."

"Aye, aye," Dick said, saluting. "Hopefully we didn't hit an iceberg."

By the time Dora and Dick reached the lobby, the ringing had stopped. Half a dozen guests had already congregated around the front desk. Some were in pajamas, others in bathrobes and, in the case of Donna Gamble, a bath towel. Barefoot in boxer shorts and t-shirt, brandishing a golf club in his right hand, Norm Gamble demanded, "What's going on?"

"No need for the golf club unless you want to practice your putting in the parlor," Dick said. "Everything is under control."

"Under control?! What if this racket starts again?"

"Ringing bells are not a racket," Nancy Peale said. She was standing in the back wearing a bathrobe that came down to her feet.

"Well, they weren't playing a lullaby."

"Look," Dora said in a commanding voice. "Dick is going to find out what caused the ringing. Can I offer anyone something to drink – a cup of tea or hot chocolate?"

"Let me help you," Terry Tarantella offered. She was wearing sweatpants and t-shirt, while Natalya had on a hoodie sweatshirt that came down to her knees.

"I'll have a scotch," Norm said plopping himself in one of the chairs. Donna, clutching the towel around her, carefully sat on the arm of the chair.

"Everyone stay calm while I go and check things out," Dick said over his shoulder while he walked through the parlor to a door that led to what had once been the sanctuary of the former church. It was pitch black and he didn't know where the light switch was. Fortunately, he had his cellphone with him and turned on its flashlight. The space was now used for events, and where there had once been pews, there were now folding chairs and card tables. Dick swept the room with the feeble light. On one of the tables was a thermos bottle and four paper coffee cups. "Someone's been here and I don't think it was for a midnight poker game," he said to Watson, who had roused himself from his slumber at the foot of the Carlsons' bed to join Dick.

Dick made his way to the double doors at the rear with Watson behind him. He opened the doors and entered the vestibule, which had been the church's narthex. The steeple was directly over him. A door in the corner of the vestibule provided access to a staircase to the choir loft and to a room where the ropes for the bells hung down through an opening in the ceiling. The door was ajar. "You stay here, Watson," Dick said, then slipped through the opening and climbed the stairs as quietly as possible. At the top he walked over to the door to the bell room. The door was closed but light seeped through the crack under it. He paused a minute, wishing he'd asked Norm to lend him his golf club, then opened the door.

Standing in the room was Cedric Thistlewaite along with two other men and a woman. Dick recognized them as members of the Eidolonic Society who were staying at the inn. The woman held a microphone in one hand attached to a recorder in the other and was wearing headphones that covered her ears. Cedric held a large flashlight and was looking up through the opening from which the bell ropes dangled.

Surprised, Dick asked Cedric what he was doing there.

Cedric lowered his flashlight, irritated at the interruption, and looked at Dick. "Same thing as you, trying to find the phantom bellringer."

"You didn't ring them?"

"Now why would we be ringing bells in the middle of the night? If you hadn't come barging in, we might have discovered the spirit behind this."

"I suspect whoever rang these bells is more likely to have been consuming spirits."

"In other words, you're only looking for the usual suspects," Cedric answered dismissively.

Ignoring Cedric's disparaging remark as to his detecting abilities, Dick asked, "How did you get up here so fast if you weren't behind all of this?"

"I and my fellow Eidolonic Society members, Gerard, Vincent and Marilyn," Cedric said, nodding at the three people, "have been keeping a vigil for any paranormal activity. We were positioned in the former sanctuary, so when we heard the bells, we immediately went into action and were able to get up here in no time."

"Two minutes and thirty-one seconds, to be exact," Vincent said, holding up his left wrist to show a watch with 2:31 blinking on its digital display.

"Unfortunately, we still weren't fast enough. The bells stopped ringing just before we entered this room," Cedric sighed. "We'll have to work on our response time."

"I've been making an audio recording of everything," Marilyn said. She had pulled the headphones down around her neck. "We keep the audio recorder on all the time when we're on watch. We might pick up an EVP."

"EVP?" Dick asked.

"Electronic voice phenomena," Cedric explained. "Those are sounds that the human ear can't pick up."

"I've been recording the temperature in here," Vincent said. "I think there was a dip right under the opening in the ceiling where Cedric is standing, but I'll have to look at the readout."

"I wouldn't be surprised if there was. This is a draughty place," Dick said, shivering.

"Our instruments are very sensitive, so we will be able to tell the difference," Cedric replied.

"Did you see anything with your flashlight?" Dick asked.

"I wasn't just looking, I was attempting to communicate. If you hold the flashlight out sometimes they will answer questions by turning it on and off. On is a yes and off is a no."

"Any luck?"

"No," Cedric answered, switching the flashlight off.

"We've also been taking readings with this EMF meter to see if there are any disturbances of the electromagnetic field," Gerard tapped a device in a holster attached to his belt. "I can't wait to download all this data onto the computer."

***

The guests looked at Dick expectantly as he entered the parlor along with Watson followed by Cedric and his team laden with their equipment.

"Did you find out who was ringing the damn bells?" demanded Norm, an empty glass of scotch in his hand.

"We won't know what's causing the paranormal activity until we examine the data we collected," Cedric answered, then added, "Science can't be rushed."

"You think it's a ghost that's causing this?" Norm asked.

"It's more likely bats did this than ghosts," Dick said. "We know there are some bats in the belfry, so they more than likely flew into the bells."

"Bats!" Donna Gamble gasped.

"Not here where we are, inside the inn, but way up on top of the steeple," Dora answered, calmly.

"I'm pretty sure that Mr. Thistlewaite and his crew of ghost hunters scared the bats away," Dick added.

"We're not ghost hunters, we're paranormal investigators," Cedric said, not hiding his irritation at Dick. "We need to examine the scientific evidence before concluding that bats are the cause rather than paranormal phenomena."

"What if it's zombies," Natalya said.

"Cool," Trevor said. "Instead of the walking dead, they're the ringing dead. This could be even better than my Zombie Apocalypse video game."

"It's not zombies, or ghosts," Dick declared. "It's just a few bats."

"They're not vampire bats are they?" Gerald Digby asked.

"This is Ilwaco not Transylvania," Dick snapped. "The only vampires we get here are on Halloween."

Dora gave Dick a cease-and-desist look and suggested that everyone go back to their rooms. "We're extending the hours for breakfast until 11 a.m. so everyone can sleep in," she added.

"How can anyone sleep with bats or ghosts whizzing about?" Donna Gamble grumbled.

As people shuffled out of the parlor, Cedric stopped next to Dick and said, "We're not going to be sleeping but looking at the data we collected. I must say that I'm a little disappointed in you. I thought as a criminologist you would follow the science rather than jump to the conclusion that it was bats."

Dick stopped himself before he said I follow the science not pseudo-science and, instead, he smiled weakly and in his best customer friendly voice, replied, "Of course, we should follow the science. As a scientist I think that we need to look at the most probable explanation based on the evidence we have so far, and since there are bats in our belfry, they're the most likely culprits."

After Cedric left, Nancy Peale walked up to Dick. She was the last guest in the parlor and had been standing quietly, unnoticed, in the shadows. "You really think that bats rang the bells?" she asked.

"It's only a theory, of course," Dick answered. "But I think you'll agree that bats is a much more probable explanation than ghosts."

"Yes," Nancy nodded, thoughtfully. "Still, it baffles me as to how bats would ring the bells using a surprise method."

"Surprising, yes, but I wouldn't say there was a method to their batty bellringing."

"No, what I mean is that the bells were rung using a method, which is what we call a sequence in change ringing, and the method is called surprise. In fact, it sounded like they were ringing *Cambridge Surprise.*"

"I'd say it was more like Sahalee Surprise," Dick replied then reached for a glass and the bottle of scotch on the bar.

CHAPTER FIVE

"I actually like the idea of ghosts," Dora said, nursing a cup of herbal tea as she sat in the parlor with Dick after the guests had gone back to their rooms. "An old inn with ghosts has cachet, but one with bats is ... is ..." She shook her shoulders in a shiver, sloshing some tea into the saucer. "Of course, the ghosts have to be polite and considerate of our guests."

"Like Casper the friendly ghost," Dick answered. He was leaning against the bar with a glass of scotch he'd poured from the bottle that Norm had nearly emptied. "Not those nasty poltergeists that would disturb our guests' slumber by ringing bells in the middle of the night."

"You need to get to the bottom of this, Dick."

"In this case it's the top not the bottom, since it's in the steeple."

Dora was not amused and replied sternly, "You know what I mean. We can't have bells ringing in the middle of the night whether they're being rung by ghosts or bats."

"Maybe it's neither."

"What do you mean?"

"According to Nancy Peale, the bells were playing a tune."

"It didn't sound like any tune I've heard."

"She didn't say tune, exactly, she said method. Apparently that's what change ringers like her call the particular sequences in which bells are rung. She said what was being rung sounded like a method with the name *Cambridge Surprise.*"

Intrigued, Dora asked, "So, you're saying that what sounded like random bell ringing was actually something called a method?"

Dick nodded. "To quote Polonius in Hamlet, 'Though this be madness, yet there is method in it.' I would say that eliminates bats as the culprits."

"It still doesn't eliminate ghosts. We could be haunted by some dead change ringer," Dora said.

"I think we should eliminate the natural suspects before we assume any supernatural ones," Dick answered.

"Maybe one of the members of the Campanology Club was just practicing?" Dora offered, then sipped her tea.

Dick jiggled his glass as he considered Dora's suggestion. "Ringing bells instead of burning the oil at midnight – now that's a lead worth pursuing."

"Then you need to speak with the Gary Dinger, the president of the Campanology Club, first thing tomorrow. Tell him what happened and warn him that if it happens again they'll have to find a new place to ring their bells."

"Me?"

"Of course, you, dear. I'm busy running an inn, and after all, you agreed to get rid of the bats ..."

"But Lars is going to do that," Dick interrupted.

"I was just going to say that since Lars is going to get rid of the bats you have time to get rid of this rogue ringer. All of our guests are booked for the week, and we certainly don't want them deciding to leave and asking for a refund, or even worse, giving us a bad rating." Dora finished her tea, smiled at Dick and said, "But I'm not worried because I have one of the world's greatest criminologists on the case."

"Yes, honey, you can rest easy," Dick replied forcing a return smile.

Dora stood up. "That's exactly what I plan on doing. I'm going to bed right now."

"I'll be up right up after I finish my scotch." As soon as Dora left the parlor, Dick picked up the bottle and poured the remaining scotch into his glass, then sat down in one of the chairs.

***

The next morning, Dora told Dick that Gary Dinger was in the parlor. Dick walked into the parlor. "Just the man I want to see," Dick said to the man sitting with Nancy Peale. "Someone rang the bells in our steeple last night, waking us all up."

"The bells woke me up as well," Gary replied. "My house is a block from here, so I am guessing a lot of other people in town heard them as well. Those bells carry quite a distance. I thought it sounded like change ringing and Nancy just confirmed it."

"It was *Cambridge Surprise*," Nancy added.

"That means whoever did it wasn't some random rope-puller," Dick said.

"Yes, it had to be someone who knew change ringing," Gary agreed.

Dick stroked his chin as if in deep thought. He still missed the professorial goatee that he had grown years ago but shaved off when Dora told him it made him look like a billy goat. "You said you were asleep when the bells were ringing?"

Gary nodded. "Since I often dream about change ringing, it took me a minute to realize that the bells that were ringing weren't inside my head."

"What about the other members of your club, were they asleep as well?"

"How would I know? Just because we ring together doesn't mean we sleep together."

"Perhaps one of your members could have snuck into the steeple and was having a little midnight practice session," Dick suggested.

"You can't practice change ringing by yourself," Gary Dinger snapped in irritation. "You have eight bells in your steeple and we use all of them in the methods we perform. Each bell needs one ringer so that would mean eight of our ten members would have had to sneak up into your steeple at midnight to practice. Besides, *Cambridge Surprise* isn't even in our repertoire so what would be the point in practicing it. That doesn't make sense."

Dick was about to utter his favorite quote from Sherlock Holmes, "When you have eliminated all which is impossible, then whatever remains, however improbable, must be the truth," when he was interrupted by Martin.

"Sorry to disturb you, Mr. Carlson, but do you want Lars to remove the speakers as well as the bats?"

Dick turned to Martin. "What speakers?"

"The ones in the steeple. They've been there for years. When this was still a church, they installed a loudspeaker system."

"Why would they do that?"

"They didn't have anyone who really knew how to ring the bells, so they hooked the loudspeakers up to an amplifier and a record player and they played records of ringing church bells. They were never removed when the church was sold and converted into an inn, and this might be a good time since Lars is up there putting in bat traps."

"Does the system still work?" Dick asked.

"I don't know. We've never had to use it."

"Where are the record player and amplifier located?"

"They're in a large closet in the foyer next to the entrance to the former sanctuary. It was used as a cloakroom when this was a church, but we use it to store chairs and tables. I suppose we should get rid of the sound system equipment as well."

"I'd like to see it first," Dick said. "They could be connected to our mysterious bell ringing."

Gary asked if he could join Dick and they both followed Martin who led them to the storage closet off the foyer of the former sanctuary. "We really need to come up with a name for the space, other than the 'former sanctuary,'" Dick said. "Something with a nautical rather than ecclesiastical ring to it, like 'snug harbor.'" He'd suggest it to Dora.

When Martin opened the door, the storage closet was filled with folding chairs. They cleared enough of them out so they could enter. At the rear of the closet was a cabinet. Martin opened the doors of the cabinet revealing an amplifier and a record turntable. The old analog dials on the amplifier were lit up. "It's on!" Martin said with surprise. "And there's a record on the turntable." He removed the record and held it up in the light of the single bulb dangling from the ceiling. "The record title is *Here We Go A Ringing: Christmas Carols on the Carillon*. There's *Silent Night* and other carols." He handed the record to Dick.

Dick looked at both sides of the record. "No *Cambridge Surprise*."

"Change ringing is completely different than a carillon," Gary explained. "A carillon has a keyboard and when you punch the keys, and you actually use your fists, a clapper strikes a bell, while in change ringing you pull on ropes that swing the bells causing the clappers to hit their sides. They sound totally different."

"In any case, those weren't Christmas carols we heard in our not-so-silent midnight," Dick said.

"I guess this is what you detectives call a lead that didn't pan out," Martin observed drily.

"Speaking of which, I wonder where that leads?" Dick asked, pointing at a wire extending from the back of the amplifier. He followed the wire, pulling folding chairs out of the way, until it disappeared behind the open closet door. Pulling on the door so that it partially closed, Dick reached down and picked up a small black box. "It's a digital recorder." He pushed the tiny play button and ringing bells, sounding a bit tinny, filled the closet.

"That's *Cambridge Surprise*!" Gary exclaimed, "Someone rigged this to play over the loudspeakers in the steeple. That's what you heard," Gary said with a smirk on his face. "I told you our members would never do something like that."

"It was only a hypothesis not an accusation," Dick said. "But someone did it."

"I don't know who did it, but I know how to stop it from happening again," Martin said, unplugging the amplifier and pulling it out of the cabinet, "and that's to get rid of this thing and the loudspeakers in the steeple."

Dick reported back to Dora on the discovery of the source of the ringing bells. "There won't be any more chimes at midnight," he added, unable to resist the reference to Shakespeare's *Henry IV*. "The cabinet with the amplifier is no longer in the closet and Lars will be removing the loudspeakers from the steeple."

"I just don't understand why someone would do this. I haven't done anything to upset anyone," Dora said, then looked at Dick and added, "and you haven't been here long enough."

CHAPTER SIX

Dick drank his second cup of coffee as he sat at a table in the dining room thinking about his next move. Dora came through the door leading from the kitchen and sat down across from him. She wasn't happy.

"This can't continue," she announced.

"I'm almost done with my coffee and I'll get right to work on the 'Chimes at Midnight Caper.'"

"What are you talking about, Dick?"

"That's the name I've given the case of who played the ringing bells through the speakers in our steeple."

"I'm not talking about that. I'm talking about breakfast."

"It's over so what is there to continue?"

"It isn't up to our standards."

"I thought it was great."

"You would. All you have for breakfast is a bagel and cream cheese, but our guests expect more than that."

"But we also serve croissants and yogurt along with bananas and oranges. That's all you need for a continental breakfast."

"People here expect something heartier."

"You mean one of those lumberjack breakfasts? We could include an axe so they can waddle out and chop down some redwoods when they're done."

Dora chuckled, "There aren't any redwoods here, this isn't California. But seriously, Dick, we need to serve something like omelets and French toast."

"You make a delicious omelet and French toast, dear."

"Me?"

"Oh, you want me to cook?"

Dora waved both hands to signal no way. "This is no time to experiment on our guests."

"You said I make a mean peanut butter and jelly sandwich."

"A PB & J is not cooking. No, we need to find someone who actually knows how to cook."

"Didn't Martin mention that the previous owner had a cook?"

"Mrs. Teal," Dora answered. "I already asked him about her, and he said that she had moved to Seattle to be closer to her daughter. I suppose I could advertise, but you never know what you'll get."

"I know someone."

"You know a cook?"

"I met a young woman yesterday who works in the bakery-cafe next to the bookstore."

"You mean the Grist and Grind on the waterfront? I've been thinking of trying some of their pastries for our breakfast."

"That's the place. Her name is Nicole. She said she wants to open a restaurant and asked if we were going to reopen the one that used to be here."

"Can she cook?"

"I tried a brownie that she baked and it was pretty good," Dick replied, leaving out that he'd told Nicole he was taking it back for Dora.

"I suppose there's nothing to lose by talking to her. In fact, I think I'll go there right now." She slapped the table with her hands and got up.

After Dora left, Dick finished his coffee and walked into the kitchen. The kitchen was quite impressive with a six-burner stove, large oven with double doors, a walk-in freezer, and other equipment. All that was missing was a cook. As he tried to picture Nicole there, dressed in white with one of those silly chef hats, he spotted Elspeth who was loading the dishes into the commercial dishwasher.

"Room for this mug?" Dick asked her.

Elspeth turned around, startled. "Oh, it's you Dr. Carlson …"

"Please call me Dick."

"Sorry, I forgot, Dick. Anyway, you gave me a bit of a scare."

"We did have quite a scare last night when the bells started ringing."

Elspeth took Dick's mug and replied. "Martin told me. He said it woke up all the guests, but it turned out to be a recording of music playing over the old loudspeaker system."

Suddenly they were interrupted by Norm Gamble, who pushed open the swinging door, "Would someone come out and take our order for breakfast?" he demanded.

"I'm afraid breakfast is over," Elspeth answered politely.

"What do you mean over, it's only ..." he looked at the Rolex on his wrist and added, "It's only 11:15."

"I imagine it is since I'm sure your Rolex is very accurate," Dick said.

"It should be for twelve grand."

Dick looked at the twenty-dollar Timex watch on his wrist. It had exactly the same time.

"Breakfast is usually served from 8-10 a.m.," Elspeth said. "But it was extended to 11 for this morning, so it ended fifteen minutes ago."

"Well, after all the racket last night that kept us up, you should extend the hours until noon."

"You'll be happy to know that we found out what caused the bell ringing, and it won't happen again," Dick said.

"Not that racket. We weren't asleep then." Norm gave an exaggerated wink. "I'm talking about the noises from the room next door, just down the hall from ours. Like somebody was stomping back and forth. Donna couldn't get any sleep and she needs her beauty sleep."

"There's no one in the room next to yours," Elspeth replied. "Maybe it was a squirrel or raccoon that got in through an open window."

"Yes, that's the most plausible explanation," Dick said. "I'll get Lars to check it out."

"Plausible like when you said last night that it was bats who were ringing the bells. That guy at the front desk ..."

"Martin."

"Yeah, well he said it turned out it wasn't bats, but some recording playing over a loudspeaker in the steeple."

"I admit that we eliminated the bats as the culprits, but investigations are a process of elimination so, in your case, we should start with what is most plausible before we jump to the conclusion that someone is stomping around inside a vacant room."

"Okay, but while you're doing your investigation can we get some breakfast even if it's after 11?"

Dick looked at Elspeth and said, "I'm sure that we can accommodate our guests, can't we?"

Elspeth quickly said to Norm, "We serve a continental breakfast of bagels with cream cheese, croissants, yogurt or fruit."

"Continental, huh? Well in this part of the continent breakfast means eggs, sausage, bacon, hash browns, pancakes."

"I'm afraid that's all we serve," Elspeth replied calmly.

"Okay," Norm growled. "Just bring it to our table."

"Which items do you want?"

"All of it, and plenty of coffee."

"You got it," Dick said. "And now I've got to get going."

Dick related Norm's complaint to Martin at the front desk. "He must have been hearing things since Elspeth says the room next to theirs is vacant."

"It could have come from the space inside the walls and it sounded to them as if it was coming from the room next door," Martin replied.

"What space inside the walls?"

"When they renovated the old church into the inn they created spaces between the outside walls and inside walls where they put the utilities like water and heating pipes for the rooms so they would be hidden."

"How much dead space are we talking about?"

"Oh, about three feet and we refer to it as utility space not dead space.."

Although Dick liked the sound of dead space, he said, "Whatever we call it, from what you're telling me a person could walk around the entire building in this space between the interior walls of the rooms and the exterior wall?"

Martin shook his head, "Not exactly. You'd have to crawl where there's a window. You no doubt noticed that all of the windows in the rooms are set in alcoves with a window seat. They had to be set back that way because of the utility space."

"And I thought it was so guests could sit there contemplating the harbor."

"That's what a window seat is for, but under the cushion is a panel that can be lifted up in order to access the utility space in case we need to make plumbing repairs."

Dick's eyes lit up. "In other words, someone could enter and exit this dead space by lifting the window seats. They could even use it to access other rooms."

"I suppose if they knew about it, and they were skinny and agile enough to get around the pipes and whatnot."

"It could explain the footsteps that Norm Gamble and his wife heard," Dick said.

"But who on earth would want to walk around between the walls?" Martin asked.

"A cat burglar, only in this case a gopher burglar, since they're going down one hole and popping up in another."

"We've never had a burglary here!" Martin exclaimed with alarm.

"I was speaking only hypothetically, Martin," Dick said. "If the way you access this space is through these hatches under the window seats of the guest rooms, and if those footsteps they heard wasn't a burglar or a ghost, they would have to have been one of our guests."

"Perhaps one of them discovered it by chance and just decided to go exploring?" Martin said. "Although, I have to admit it doesn't seem probable that they would do it in the middle of the night."

"Maybe we have a sleep walker on the loose."

***

When Dora returned, Dick filled her in on the mysterious footsteps and the dead space between the walls. "The most logical explanation is that one of our guests found the access hatch under the window seat and decided to go on a post-midnight stroll."

"Oh dear," she sighed, then her face brightened. "But it's probably only a one-time occurrence. I mean, whoever it was will have done their exploring and that's that."

"That would be that unless it's the same person who played the recording of the bells."

"You're saying that one of our guests did that as well?"

"I'm not saying that they're actually connected, I'm just hypothesizing that they could be."

"Well, you need to stop hypothesizing and find out who it is. We can't have this person continuing to disturb our guests or, even worse, robbing them. Our guests should feel safe and secure during their stay."

"We have a sanctuary and they're supposed to be safe places," Dick offered.

"It's been deconsecrated, or whatever they do when they close a church."

"Maybe they forgot? I mean, did we get something that stated it was deconsecrated when we bought the place?"

"There was nothing like that mentioned in any of the documents."

"Then for all we know the consecration hasn't been cancelled and the sanctuary is still covered by a divine warranty."

Dora gave Dick a playful punch on the right arm. "Really, Dick, this is no joking matter."

"Who's joking?"

"Enough, Dick," Dora said firmly. "On another more pleasant subject, I spoke with Nicole and we agreed on a plan. Instead of hiring her as an employee we will let her use the kitchen for her catering business and in return she will make breakfast for our guests."

"I didn't know she had a catering business."

"She would like to until she can open a restaurant, but she needs a proper kitchen."

"Is she quitting her job at the Grist and Grind?"

"Not until her catering business takes off. She said she would change her hours there so she can make breakfast. We're going to meet here at 1 p.m. so she can check out the kitchen and come up with a menu. She'll do the shopping for everything that is needed for breakfasts, and we will reimburse her. Also, we agreed that she'll keep a ledger with an inventory and an ongoing tally of what she uses. We can check the pantry and refrigerator any time to make sure that everything is accounted for."

"Unless our mystery person makes a midnight raid on the refrigerator."

Dora froze. "Oh my. Nicole said that she would need to use the kitchen at night to do the cooking for her catering business.

What if she hears some strange noises like the Gambles did? I suppose we should tell her about these ..."

"Unexplained noises?"

"Yes, noises but leave out unexplained since we're sure there's some innocent explanation."

"We are?"

"Well, I am, because I'm not a criminologist like you are who sees everything as the work of a criminal. In any case, we want to reassure her, not scare her half to death. After all, no real harm has been done. We can tell her that there are all sorts of night noises in a creaky, drafty old building like this, especially with the winds we get here."

"Those weren't wind chimes we heard from the steeple last night," Dick said.

Dora stared at him, then snapped, "On second thought, maybe it's better if I talk to her without you."

"I couldn't agree more, dear."

CHAPTER SEVEN

Morgan Murray's boat, *Hard to Fathom*, wasn't hard to find even though there was a sea of boats in the Ilwaco Harbor. After five minutes navigating the web of floating docks, Dick spotted the name painted on the stern of a fishing boat. The boat looked like it had spent most of its time being battered around the Bering Sea – not that Dick had ever been to the Bering Sea, but he'd seen a reality television show about people fishing there that made him seasick. The wheelhouse was near the bow followed by a low cabin and then a long deck that ended with a stubby stern. There were some poles on the deck that projected straight up into the air like antennae. Dick suspected they were for catching very large fish in very deep water.

He stood on the dock, staring at the narrow gangplank, wondering what the protocol was for boarding, when a man emerged from the cabin door who could have been an Ernest

Hemingway impersonator with a salt and pepper beard and an old gray wool turtleneck sweater stretched over his barrel chest.

"You want to go charter fishing?" the man yelled.

"Nope," Dick yelled back.

"Then are you trying to convert me to some religion or sell me something I don't need?"

Dick held up his copy of *Unsolved Mysteries of Cape Disappointment.*

"I don't give refunds."

"I don't want a refund, I'd like you to sign my copy."

"In that case, come on board," the man said, then rang a small bell attached to the cabin.

Dick walked the plank onto the deck and said, "This boat looks like it's done some serious fishing at one time."

"Aye, it has," Morgan replied, casting his eyes around the deck. "She's a trawler that was built for commercial fishing, which is what I did with her for thirty-odd years. There used to be winches on the stern for lowering and raising the net that was towed behind it. It's small for a trawler, but bigger than most charter boats, which is what I use her for now. Lots of deck space so people don't bump into each other, which can happen a lot in the rough seas we get around here."

"What made you stop commercial fishing?"

"The boat needed major work done, so I brought her to the shipyard here. While I was overhauling her, I sort of overhauled myself. Since I was interested in local history, I volunteered at the Cape Disappointment Heritage Museum, and they asked me to put together an exhibit on ships that had wrecked at Cape Disappointment. It seems it was a big success, so they asked me if I could write a booklet on it that they could sell at the gift store. Turned out to be a bestseller for them, so then they asked me to do another one on shipwrecks. I found that I liked writing about shipwrecks a hell of a lot more than trying to escape them. I've been writing books for five years now and expanded my subject matter beyond shipwrecks."

"And you've expanded the places where your books are sold," Dick said. "I bought my copy at Ballast Books. The owner not only promoted your book, she told me where I could find you for an autograph."

"Aye, Tillie is one of my biggest fans. Unfortunately," Morgan sighed, "while switching careers from fishing to writing books no doubt added to my longevity, it didn't do the same for my income. That's why I supplement it with some charter fishing. People pay me to watch them fish," he laughed. "And they supply the beer. Speaking of which, how about joining me in one. A beer is good for what ails you."

"It's a little early for me," Dick said.

"It's a little late for me. I got up at four so I could take some folks from Seattle out at five on a half-day charter. Why don't we compromise and we'll split a bottle?"

Without waiting for an answer, Morgan ducked through the cabin entrance. Through the doorway Dick could see Morgan opening a small refrigerator, that together with a two-burner stove and sink comprised the galley. To the left of the galley there were several steps leading to a door that Dick assumed provided access to the enclosed wheelhouse. There was another door to the right of the galley and Dick wondered if this led to Morgan's living quarters.

Morgan returned on deck with an open bottle of Cape D Dark Ale and poured half into a glass he'd brought with him. He held them up in either hand. "You want the bottle or the glass?"

"Glass is fine, thanks," Dick replied and took the glass, which on closer inspection looked as if its main use was for rinsing out Morgan's mouth after he brushed his teeth. Not that brushing his teeth had made much difference judging from what Dick saw when Morgan opened his mouth.

"Have a seat," Morgan said, motioning to a swivel chair bolted to the deck. After Dick was seated, Morgan sat down opposite him in another swivel chair. "To unsolved mysteries," he said, hoisting the bottle and taking a hearty swig.

Dick lifted the glass in a return toast then took a sip. It wasn't bad even with the hint of toothpaste. "Now, if you give me the book I'll sign it."

Dick handed him the book as well as a pen.

After Morgan took another swig of beer, he put down his bottle and took the book and the pen. "What's your name so I can make it personal?"

"Dick Carlson."

"You the Carlson who now runs the Sahalee Inn?"

"My wife runs it. I just try to keep from getting run over. I'm a criminologist."

"A criminologist, you don't say," Morgan said and then held up the book. "I suppose you being a criminologist these unsolved mysteries really interest you."

"In particular your chapter, 'Murder at Sahalee Inn' that involves an unsolved murder. Although I was surprised to learn after reading it that the murder was committed in a house that used to be next to the Sahalee Inn or, to be historically accurate, where the Ilwaco Community Church was before it was sold and converted into the Sahalee Inn."

Morgan winked and smiled, "I admit I took a bit of literary license, but everything else is completely accurate based on my research, which, if I say so myself, was meticulous. The murder victim was the church's minister, Reverend Isaac Wigglesworth, and they never found out who did it."

Dick raised his right eyebrow and noted in a skeptical voice, "Who, according to your meticulous research, could have been a ghost."

Morgan chuckled and started scribbling something on the title page of the book. "I only wrote that some people suspected it was the ghost of Captain Johnson who killed Wigglesworth then burned down the house."

"Do you actually believe that?"

"What I believe, based on my research, is that some people suspected it was a ghost. You should be pleased at the possibility, since people like to stay in places that might have a ghost."

"I think our guests would prefer a friendly ghost."

Morgan laughed. "I'll admit Captain Johnson certainly wasn't friendly when he was alive. From the accounts we have he was a tight-fisted bastard who made a lot of enemies. He was one of the first pilots who guided ships across the treacherous Columbia Bar and he charged a pretty penny for his services."

"You write in the book that many people believed that gold was stolen from a ship that ran aground off Sand Island while he was piloting it."

"Sand Island is right over there," Morgan pointed toward an island in the distance beyond the Harbor entrance. "Back then it was farther away, in the middle of the Columbia, but it's moved this way over the years. Well, it is sand so you'd hardly think it would stay in one place. Anyway, the ship he was piloting ran aground on the island during a gale, broke up and sank. Johnson managed to swim to the island. Everyone else on board the ship drowned. Being the pilot not the captain he wasn't obliged to go down with the ship."

"You also write that people thought he wrecked the ship on purpose so he could get the gold, and that he buried it on the island and then came back, dug it up, and hid it in his house."

"Yep," Morgan said with a nod. "Supposedly he stashed it in the big house he'd built. After he was rescued from Sand Island, he stopped entertaining visitors, not that he was much of a host before. Even after he married a Chinook woman and they had some children, he wouldn't let her and their kids live in the house. Instead, he kept them in a large one room addition he constructed behind it. People figured he didn't want anyone in the house because he was afraid they'd find the gold. After he drowned when the boat he was sailing over to Astoria capsized – something that seemed pretty fishy considering how good a skipper he was and that he was a good swimmer – they searched all over the house looking for the gold but couldn't find it. Shortly after that some of the finer and more pious citizens of Ilwaco bought the house and surrounding property so they could build a church on it. They hired Reverend Wigglesworth to be the pastor and he lived in the house. The addition behind it was converted into space for worship services until they finished constructing the church next door."

Dick nodded his head, "And then the house burned down and they found the charred remains of Reverend Wigglesworth with his head bashed in."

"Exactly," Morgan said. "Based on the evidence, the inquest concluded that he was murdered and the fire intentionally set. Since Wigglesworth was too new to the area to have made any enemies – other than the Devil, of course, otherwise he could hardly be called a man of God – the most logical motive for the murder was that by burning down the house it would be easier for the killer to find the hidden gold. One advantage of gold over paper currency being that it isn't combustible. Wigglesworth just happened to be in the way. Guess you could say he wasn't able to wiggle out of it."

When Morgan stopped chuckling at his own joke, Dick observed, "You write in your book that if the murderer planned to sift through the ruins of the house he was thwarted by the church congregation who soon covered it with several feet of dirt.

"Exactly," Morgan replied. "They covered it up after they collected whatever remains of Reverend Wigglesworth they could locate in the smoldering ruin and buried them six feet under in Ilwaco Cemetery. Of course, the Reverend was mostly cremated by the fire so there wasn't much to recover other than his bashed in skull and a few other bones. Would have been hard to tell what ashes were human, so they probably missed a lot of the Reverend and trusted God to put him back together in the hereafter. Anyway, they then continued expeditiously with the construction of the church."

"But they never found the person who murdered Reverend Wigglesworth and burned down the house," Dick said.

"Nope," Morgan said, shaking his head. "Bad for justice, but good for me since otherwise it wouldn't be an unsolved mystery."

"I'm starting to think of it more as a cold case."

"As cold as a corpse," Morgan replied. "A corpse being what the murderer would be now, unless he was already dead to begin with, which some people started to believe. Like I said earlier, they believed that Johnson's ghost committed the foul deed because he was afraid that Wigglesworth would find the gold and use it to help fund the building of the church. Since Johnson was an upstanding citizen of hell, he couldn't stand to see his loot used that way, so he got the Devil to send him back as a ghost to burn down the house. You could say that killing a Reverend was a bonus."

"I would say that explanation is not just far-fetched, it's completely out of this world."

"I don't believe it myself, but I put it in the book because that's what some people believed at the time." Morgan signed his name under what he had written on the title page, closed the book and handed it back to Dick.

Dick took the book, finished his beer and then said, "It's hard to believe that no one tried to find the buried gold after the church was built."

"The church didn't want to look for it and didn't want anyone else digging holes in their holy ground."

"What about after the church sold the property and it was converted to an inn?"

Morgan shrugged his broad shoulders. "Probably because the whole thing was forgotten by then. Anyway, nobody dug up anything."

"You mean as far as you know."

Morgan laughed and dropped his empty beer bottle into a bucket next to his swivel chair. "It's hard to keep something like that a secret around here, and if someone dug up the property where the house had been and found a hoard of gold coins, with all due modesty, I'd know. Of course, now that you own the inn, you're free to start digging."

"You said the church was built near the house. Would you happen to know the precise location of the house?"

"Let's see," Morgan answered, scratching his beard. "I'd have to consult my archive on that."

"You have an archive?"

"Yep, an historian isn't worth his salt without an archive, and I'm an old salt."

"Is it very far?"

"You're sitting on top of it."

"What?"

Morgan slapped his beefy thighs with his hands and got to his feet. "It's in the hold below you." He went to a hatch on the deck and pulled it open. The hatch cover flopped on the deck with a resounding thud. He turned and told Dick to watch his step as he followed him down the ladder then disappeared into the hold.

After they descended the ladder, Morgan switched on an overhead light revealing a room that appeared to be as long and wide as the deck above. There were shelves on either side with cardboard boxes on them, everything infused by the smell of fish. "This used to be the refrigerated hold when it was a trawler. If it smells fishy down here it's because this is where the fish I caught were stored. It would be hard to get rid of the smell even if I wanted to and I don't get many visitors down here."

Now let's see," Morgan said as he looked at the labels on the boxes. "I think what we're looking for is in here." He pulled a box off the shelf, then placed it on a metal table. After rummaging through the contents he pulled out a sheaf of papers. Depositing the box on the floor he spread the papers on the table. "These are copies of the survey for the property. The original is in the County Courthouse. I reduced them from their original size when I made the copies so you need to look closely."

He bent over one of the sheets. "According to this they built the church just east of where the house was." He placed another sheet next to the first. "They did a major renovation of the church in 1915 when Ilwaco was booming with fishing, canneries, and the timber industry. They enlarged the sanctuary, built a taller steeple with more bells, and constructed this addition here." He pointed a stubby finger at a building outline. "The addition is where the inn's rooms are now, so I'd say the inn is right up against where the original house was. In fact," he looked from one sheet to the other, "it looks like they built part of the addition on top of where the house stood."

"The Inn doesn't have a basement," Dick said.

"Then they didn't do much excavation work and wouldn't have found anything that was buried where the house was," Morgan said.

"Then if Captain Johnson's treasure of gold coins is buried in the ruins of the house where Reverend Wigglesworth was murdered, it's under our inn."

CHAPTER EIGHT

Dora looked over her Sahalee Inn dominion, or at least the parlor where she was sitting with a cup of tea. Yes, it was hers. Technically, it was Dick's as well, but in this kingdom she was Queen and Dick the royal consort. A consort who previously hadn't acted too royally since he had consorted with all sorts of unsavory types while gallivanting all over the globe pursuing criminals. Now she worried if what had kept them together all this time was that they weren't together all the time. She had to admit that now that she had to concentrate on the inn, she was aware of how distracting his presence could be. Dora sipped her tea.

Probably, the late Queen Elizabeth had felt the same way about Prince Phillip, who had been her royal consort. No doubt she encouraged him to play polo and shoot grouse and hunt foxes and all those other outdoorsy things that royals do to get him out of the castle. Dick wasn't outdoorsy but he was a criminologist, and that's really just a detective with a PhD, so Dora needed to encourage him to do his detecting, but only small crimes that were local that he could solve before cocktail hour. This bell ringing business was a good example. What he needed was a tidy Agatha Christie mystery to keep him occupied, but without any murder. Dora finished her tea and went to inspect the rest of her kingdom.

***

Fortunately, Dora thought as she hit the floor five minutes later, they hadn't removed the plush carpet from Room Two. As much as she loved the hardwood floor underneath the ugly shag, it would have been a much more painful landing. On her inspection tour, she had opened the door to the ground floor room and discovered that inside it was pitch black. She had walked quickly toward the window that was faintly outlined by daylight in order to raise the shades, more than a little peeved because they should not have been lowered. That's when she felt her right foot catch on something and she landed on the floor. Rising to her hands and knees she looked around and could make out in the dim light coming from the hallway that the soft thing she had tripped over was a body. Her first thought was that it was strange that there should be a body in a vacant room, and her second thought was that she shouldn't scream because that would alarm the guests. Dora got to her feet, stepped over the body and flipped the light switch next to the door. Looking up at her was Elspeth. Dora quickly knelt down and prepared to do CPR, which she had just brushed up on in case she ever had to resuscitate a guest. Just as Dora bent over her to give the kiss of life, Elspeth's eyes opened and she asked in a groggy voice, "What happened?"

"I don't know, I just found you lying here on the floor," Dora answered, deciding to leave out the part about tripping over her body.

"Where?" Elspeth asked as Dora helped her sit up.

"Room Two."

"I remember that I heard something inside this room when I was walking to Room Three to change out the towels. The room isn't booked for tonight so nobody is supposed to be in here. The room was locked so I used my master key and opened the door..."

"And it was dark inside because the blinds were down."

"Yes, the blinds were down and I remember being mad because the light shouldn't have been left on in an unoccupied room."

"And then what?"

"Yes, and then what?" Elspeth put her right finger to her lips in deep thought. "I don't remember what happened after that."

"Were you knocked out?" Dora asked. "You might have a concussion." Dora inspected Elspeth's head, pushing her hair aside. "I don't see any blood or a bump."

"I don't have a headache so I must have fainted," Elspeth said, then patted the carpet. "Good thing we still have a carpet instead of a hardwood floor in this room or I might have broken something when I fell."

"Do you remember anything that would have caused you to faint?" Dora asked as she helped Elspeth to her feet.

Elspeth shook her head, "My mind's a blank."

"It had to have been a terrible shock to have made you faint and then not remember anything."

Elspeth gripped Dora's forearm and looked at her. "Do you think I saw the ghost?"

"What ghost?"

"Why, the one that haunts the inn!"

"You actually believe that?" Dora asked. She was a bit torn, she had to admit. On the one hand, the idea of having a ghost in residence had intrigued her. Dora wasn't dismissive of the possibility the way Dick was. In fact, she felt that she might have some sort of ESP or whatever, because she sometimes had a premonition that someone she cared about was in trouble. Usually it involved Dick who had an uncanny ability to get into trouble.

"I've heard things before and sometimes felt, you know, a presence, but I've never actually seen the ghost," Elspeth said. "I was never afraid or anything. I thought he would be some cute little ghost in a white sheet, like Casper, but if he was scary enough to make me faint, I'm not so sure..."

"You said 'he.' Does that mean what you saw was a he, not a she?"

"I don't know, Dora. For all I know Casper could be a 'she' not a 'he' under that sheet."

Dora put her arm around Elspeth's shoulders. "I imagine it was just the shock of seeing something you didn't expect, not because it was some sort of ... you know ..." Dora's voice trailed off as she looked around the room.

"Some sort of horrible ghoul?" Elspeth said, freeing herself from Dora and running into the hallway.

Dora followed her, "I was going to say some harmless apparition, although I'm sure there's an innocent explanation for the whole thing."

Elspeth crossed her arms and looked at Dora. "What I know is that until I'm sure that it wasn't a ghost I saw in there that made me keel over, I'm not stepping inside that room."

"It just so happens that a group of experts on investigating these sorts of things is staying with us for the next few days. What if I ask them to look into this?"

"Will they use one of those 'weegee' things?"

"You mean a Ouija board?" Dora remembered the Halloween slumber party at Megan Maloney's house when she was twelve. Cindy Kuperman had brought a Ouija board and suggested they hold a séance. All five of the girls sat on the floor around the board in Megan's candlelit bedroom with their hands on a piece of plastic shaped like a heart. When Cindy called on a spirit to move the piece in their hands the candle blew out and a face appeared floating in the darkness. While the other girls screamed, Dora got up and found the light switch near the door. When she turned on the lights, they revealed that the apparition belonged to Megan's older brother, Harry, who was shining a flashlight on his face. The only things summoned that night were giggles. Stashing away the memory, Dora told Elspeth, "From what I understand they use highly sophisticated, scientific equipment in their investigations."

***

"Ah, yes, this is perfect for our investigations," Cedric Thistlewaite pronounced as he surveyed the room. He had already listened patiently to Elspeth who couldn't provide much in the way of details because she had fainted. Now he and his team were crowded into the room. "It's fortuitous that this is an unoccupied room, at least by corporeal bodies. The presence of people can interfere with our highly sensitive equipment. The fact that the room is one in which paranormal phenomenon was observed such a short time ago is even better."

"We really don't know for certain that Elspeth saw a ghost," Dora said. "All we know is that she fainted. Remember how everyone was jumping to the conclusion that there were ghosts up in the steeple ringing the bells, and then my husband, Dick, discovered it was just a recording."

"You're quite right, Mrs. Carlson. As a scientist I should always wait until the data have been collected and carefully analyzed. Which is what we will begin doing as soon as our equipment is set up."

"I do hope it won't take long before you can tell us if something supernatural happened here. This is the only vacant room we have, and I don't want to turn away any potential guests. Is there some way you can speed things up? Some sort of bait you can put out?"

Cedric bristled and replied, "This isn't a fishing expedition but an important scientific investigation. All I can say is that we will stop as soon as we uncover evidence of a paranormal occurrence. It's possible we can end our investigation quickly if, in our initial sweep of the room, we pick up latent traces of recent paranormal activity."

"Latent traces?"

"Like finding fingerprints."

"I doubt you'll find any fingerprints," Dora said. "I would think that a ghost would be smart enough to wear gloves. However, I suppose you could look for their DNA. Dick says that's all the rage in forensics now. Seems like people shed more DNA than dandruff – even bald people."

"Funny that you should say that," Cedric answered, "because I just read a paper with the title 'The Afterlife of DNA.'"

"What does the paper say?"

"It's highly technical, much too complicated to explain in detail to a layperson," Cedric said dismissively. "But basically, the author postulates that since a creature's DNA survives after it has died, including creatures who died thousands of years ago and are even extinct as a species, then DNA could be a portal between this life and the next."

"Like a double helix to heaven," Dora said, suppressing the urge to hum the opening bars of *Stairway to Heaven*.

"As scientists we don't use the word heaven. Anyway, it's all theoretical at this point. Still, the paper raises the possibility of a new area for paranormal research."

"We're all set up," Marilyn announced from inside the room.

"Then everyone should leave the room so we can start," Cedric said. He turned back to Dora and asked her for the key to the room so they could lock it. "We don't want anyone to enter the room and contaminate it while the investigation is underway. Anyone living, that is."

CHAPTER NINE

As they ate lunch, Dick listened calmly to Dora while she recounted what happened to her and Elspeth. He thought it better not to tell her what he thought of the chance that Cedric Thistlewaite and his Eidolonic Society would discover that it was a ghost that caused Elspeth to faint. He didn't have to because Dora did it for him when she pointed her spoon dripping with Greek yogurt at him and declared, "I know it's nonsense that Elspeth thinks she saw a ghost, but you see, after they do their scientific mumbo jumbo and say they can't find a ghost, Elspeth will know that the room isn't haunted and she'll be willing to clean it."

Dick put down his half-eaten turkey on wheat and asked, "Didn't you say that people thinking the place might be haunted would help business?"

"Yes, but we don't want anyone to think that it's haunted by something scary enough to make people faint. We want something like that cute Casper the Friendly Ghost."

"What about the Addams Family? We could give them a group rate."

"Now, you're being silly," Dora said.

"Unlike a cute ghost in a sheet," Dick replied. "When Thistlewaite fails to uncover a ghost, won't Elspeth still want to know what it was that actually scared her?"

Dora frowned. "You're right. If we don't find some innocent explanation, I might not be able to persuade her to clean that room and we won't be able to rent it out."

"And disappoint someone who wants to stay there and spend the night with Casper."

Ignoring Dick's joke Dora said, "I'll leave finding the innocent explanation to you, darling, since you're the detective. Now, tell me what you were up to while you were out sleuthing about town."

As Dick filled her in on his visit to Morgan Murray, Dora interrupted him. "An unsolved murder and a buried treasure, and it all happened here?"

"Not exactly here because this building wasn't here then. It happened in a house that stood on this spot before they built the church, which is now the inn."

"Which is here, just like I said."

"Okay, it's here," Dick nodded in defeat.

"And according to this book, a ghost might have murdered this Reverend Wriggle...something?"

"His name was Wigglesworth," Dick said, holding up his autographed copy of *Unsolved Mysteries of Cape Disappointment.*

"If people read this book, they'll think that we have a very unfriendly ghost."

"Right," Dick nodded as sagely as he could. "Casper wouldn't be caught dead murdering someone."

Dora pointed her spoon at Dick again and said, "This isn't funny, Dick. We had a plan to put a positive spin on this whole ghost thing, and now there's this book by what's his name ..."

"Morgan Murray."

"Right, and you said he's a captain, so he has some credibility."

"Not if you saw his boat," Dick said. "Besides, I doubt that the average person is going to read his book."

"You did."

"But I'm only one person and I'm hardly your average reader to begin with."

"I agree that you're not average, otherwise I never would have married you, but we only need a few people to create problems. I mean, they could post something on social media or something," Dora replied, then put down her spoon and added, "Maybe we can buy all of his books."

"And burn them in a bonfire on the beach?"

"That would attract too much attention."

"I was joking."

"I told you this isn't funny, Dick. No, I can see that there's really only one way to stop this."

"What's that?"

"You need to prove it wasn't a ghost."

"And how do I do that?" Dick asked as he finished off his sandwich.

Dora smiled and said, "Why, dear, you just have to find out who really murdered this Reverend Wiggly Piggly that's how."

"Reverend Wiggles ..." Dick started to correct Dora again, but then stopped and said, "Finding the guilty person will put to rest this rumor that it was Captain Johnson's ghost and solve a very cold case."

"And that leaves you with three hot ones," Dora said, "The first is who woke everyone in the inn after they plugged a recording of ringing bells into the PA system in the steeple. The second is who disturbed the Gambles by pacing inside the wall of their room. And the third is who scared Elspeth."

Dick looked at Watson and said, "We've now got four games afoot, Watson, which happens to match the number of paws you have, so stop snoozing and get off your haunches."

Speaking of haunches, Dick was not someone who believed in hunches. He was, after all, a man of science who used what Hercule Poirot, the only Agatha Christie detective that was even close to his favorite Sherlock Holmes, called his brain's little grey cells. Although Dick liked to think that with all the exercise he gave them, his brain cells were larger than normal. He said to Watson who was now on his feet, "I think it would help to talk this over with another professional." Watson barked. "Yes, I know you're a professional, Watson, but it would be helpful to have someone with a human vocabulary."

***

"This looks more like a bar than a police station," Dick said to Sally Gilmore as they sat down on stools next to a long counter that still smelled of beer. "Do you serve booze when you book people?"

"It used to be a dive bar. Its name was the Dungeness, but everyone called it the Dungeon, which is appropriate since until we have a real holding cell, we're using a storage room in the basement. Since that's where they kept the beer kegs, I suppose it could be considered cruel and unusual punishment for the drunks we arrest. We just moved here a month ago from our old police station next to City Hall when it was condemned by the Building Department."

"Why here?"

"We raided this place so often that it lost its liquor license. Without the license, the place was worthless, so the owner gave it to the city as payment for the fines on all of the outstanding violations. The city decided that since the Police Department was responsible for a vacant building they now owned, we should move the Department here temporarily."

"How long is temporarily?"

"As long as it takes to pass a bond issue to build a new one, which means an increase in taxes, that's how temporarily," she replied. "Now what is it you want to discuss, or is this a social visit? If it is, we should go to a bar that still serves booze."

"Actually, I want to fill you in on some criminal activity," Dick said, then proceeded to tell her everything that had happened as Sally made notes on a legal pad.

When he had finished, Sally shook her head. "So, if I'm getting this straight, there's a murder case that's so cold it's frozen, and three cases of malicious mischief only it might not be malicious if the perpetrator is a friendly ghost."

"You left out that the murderer of Reverend Wigglesworth might be the ghost of Captain Johnson."

"A not-so-friendly ghost in that case," Sally laughed and put down her pencil. "I'm not sure what the police can do if it is or was a ghost. Even if we were able to catch and arrest a ghost, we couldn't lock him in a cell since they can walk through walls. Not to mention that if it went to trial, we'd have to go to the cemetery to get a jury of their peers." Sally grinned, "On the other hand, we don't have to worry about violating their constitutional rights. I mean, a Miranda warning for a ghost would have to be something like, 'You have the right to remain dead.'"

Dick held up both of his hands. "Don't get me wrong, I certainly don't think a ghost was the perpetrator in any of the cases."

"In Mr. Carlson's opinion, it isn't a ghost," Sally repeated as she wrote the words on the legal pad and then scratched out Mr. and wrote Dr.

"Could you add, 'In his scientific opinion as a noted criminologist'?" Dick said.

Sally added it to the end of what she wrote, then, "Anything else?"

"I suggest that we concentrate on solving the malicious mischief at our inn before anyone strikes again."

"And there's no need to worry about whoever murdered Reverend Wigglesworth striking again, since now that we've eliminated the undead, all of the suspects are dead dead," Sally said, tapping her pen on her pad.

"Right," said Dick. "We can narrow it down further to those who had an opportunity." Dick handed Sally a sheet of paper. "This is a list of guests who are staying at the inn. I've written besides each of their names some background information, most of it gleaned from personal interactions during our cocktail hour yesterday. Nothing like a stiff drink for loosening the tongue."

Sally took the sheet and sighed, "Too bad we can't reopen the bar and serve drinks to our suspects during interrogation."

As she started to look at the sheet, Dick's cellphone started ringing. The ringtone was the opening bars from the theme to the old *Dragnet* television show. Watson, who had been snoozing on the floor, was suddenly on his feet and barking. Dick pulled his phone from the inside pocket of his windbreaker as he said to Watson, "You don't have to bark every time I get a phone call that a new game may be afoot."

"How can you know that when you haven't even answered your phone?" Sally asked.

"Because I have two lines on my phone. One is my regular line and the second is a number that only people I know use to call me about cases that I might be interested investigating."

"And, of course, that's the one with the *Dragnet* ringtone," Sally said, as Dick put the phone to his ear.

CHAPTER TEN

"Is this Dick Carlson?" the man on the other end of the line demanded.

"Yes."

"I'm calling with a tip about a crime."

"What's the crime?"

"It hasn't happened yet, but it's going to happen in that place of yours."

"You mean the Sahalee Inn?"

"Yeah, the inn."

"How do you know that someone is going to commit a crime?"

"I'm the bartender at the High and Dry, and some guys I'd never seen before walked in and ordered a couple of beers. While they were drinking I overheard one of them say to the other that they might have to feed somebody to the fish, and the other one said that they'd have to cut them up into bait first, then the first one said at least they wouldn't have to buy a fishing license, and they both laughed."

"That does sound suspicious. What does the Sahalee Inn have to do with it?"

"They asked for directions to the inn so I figure that must be where this future fish bait is staying. That's also why I knew they weren't from around here since everyone knows where it is. I mean how many inns have a steeple?"

"It used to be a church."

"I know. Hey, if a church can be turned into an inn maybe I should turn my bar into a church. Business is pretty slow on Sunday mornings. I could have sunrise services and sell Bloody Marys and ..."

Dick decided to cut him off and asked, "When did you hear these guys?"

"Just a few minutes ago. As soon as I overheard what they were saying I announced to everyone in the bar that I needed to take a smoking break, and when I got outside I called the inn. Actually, I stopped smoking five years ago but they wouldn't know that. Anyway, I told a woman named Dora who said she was the innkeeper that I was calling about a crime and she said that you were the person who dealt with crime and gave me this number." The man added that he had to get back to the bar or people would be helping themselves to the booze and then hung up.

Dick relayed the conversation to Sally and asked. "Do you know this High and Dry bar?"

"I'd be a sorry excuse for a police chief if I didn't. After we closed this place, the High and Dry moved up in the rankings and is now the number one dive bar in town."

"Then you must know the bartender, the guy who called?"

"There's only one bartender, Alf," Sally said. "Alfson is his last name but everyone calls him Alf. He's also the owner but he doesn't want people to know because the place is such a pit. When people complain he says he'll pass it on to the owner. Why don't I drive you there. It's not far."

"I'd like to see if I can talk to these guys Alf overheard and that's not going to happen if I show up in a police car," Dick said.

"I can take you in our unmarked car and I'll put on my plain clothes. They're not actually plain, but you know what I mean."

"Does that mean you're also coming into the bar with me?"

"They won't recognize my face if they're not from around here. Besides, I'll put on my Lady Gaga sunglasses and let my hair down. You may need me because these guys could be armed and dangerous."

"Should we get some back up?"

"I am the back up. Besides, we have your dog, Watson." They both looked down at Watson, who barked when he heard his name.

"They allow dogs in the bar?"

"As long as they're accompanied by a paying customer. I'll just change into something more undercover."

A few minutes later Dick, Sally, and Watson stood just inside the entrance to the High and Dry as their eyes adjusted to the dim interior. "Pretty dark in here," Dick said.

"They've got a lot to hide," Sally replied, keeping her Lady Gaga sunglasses on despite the dimness.

"Those two rough looking men must be our suspects," Dick said nodding toward the two men sitting at the bar. They had turned briefly to see who had entered, before returning their attention to the beer mugs in front of them.

"They're a couple of local fishermen whose only criminal activity is catching more than the limit – that's the fishing limit, although they're known to exceed their limit in alcohol as well."

"They're the only customers in here."

"We can ask Alf," Sally answered.

A beefy man in an orange polo shirt stretched over his ample belly and greasy strands of gray hair poking out from under a Seattle Mariners baseball cap was drying a beer mug. From the look of the towel, Dick figured he was just replacing the grime. Dick announced who he was, then started to introduce Sally. Alf cut him off. "The Chief and I are well acquainted."

"This is a friendly visit," Sally said with a smile.

"That'll be a first. How about a drink to celebrate?"

"Not that friendly."

"What about your dog?" Alf asked looking over the bar at Watson. "They're supposed to be man's best friend."

"He's on the wagon, aren't you Watson," Dick said, giving Watson a pat on the head. "Where are the two men you mentioned in your phone call?"

"They left a couple of minutes after I talked to you," Alf answered.

"How about a description?"

"They were both wearing black suits and white shirts and skinny black ties. You could say they more than met our dress code: no shoes, no shirt, no service."

"I guess pants are optional," Sally deadpanned.

"I bet they were wearing sunglasses as well, like the Blues Brothers," Dick said.

"They didn't look like brothers."

"I meant John Belushi and Dan Akroyd, the comedians who called themselves the Blues Brothers because in their act they played the blues." When Alf responded with a blank stare, Dick added, "They dressed like the guys you described."

"Oh, those Blues Brothers. They looked sort of like them, now that you mention it, only these guys didn't wear black hats with the small brims like the real Blues Brothers..."

"They're called fedoras."

Alf shrugged. "I only know about baseball caps. That's all anyone wears around here." He tapped the brim of his Seattle Mariners cap. "But to answer your question, they were both wearing sunglasses when they walked in but took them off."

Sally took her Gaga glasses off and said, "It's so dim in here they wouldn't have been able to see their way to the bar if they kept them on."

"Anything else you can tell us about how they looked?" Dick asked.

"Let's see," Alf said, scratching the stubble on his chin. "One of them was about six foot tall. He had broad shoulders and his hair was cut real short so he looked almost bald. The other guy was shorter and sort of chubby with black slicked back hair."

"How old were they?"

"Hard to say. As the Chief said, it isn't very bright in here ..."

"It's not just the lighting that isn't very bright in here," Sally said.

"Look Chief, the law says I only have to check IDs, not IQs," Alf laughed then turned to Dick and said, "But to get to your question, the taller guy seemed younger than the other guy, but maybe that was because he was in better shape."

"Did they say where they were going when they left here?" Dick asked.

"Nope, but like I said, they asked where the inn was, so I figure that's where they were headed."

"You didn't happen to see what kind of vehicle they were driving, did you?" Sally asked.

"You can't exactly see out the windows here," Alf answered. "Those blinds would fall apart if I tried to raise them. All I can say is that they didn't seem to be the type who'd be driving a pickup or an RV."

Dick felt like a spelunker climbing out of a cave when he and Sally stepped outside the High and Dry. As his eyes adjusted to the sunlight, he looked at Sally, who had put her sunglasses back on. "Watson and I should go back to the inn in case those two guys show up."

"I'll drop you off and then cruise around to see if I can spot them. If Alf's description is accurate that shouldn't be hard since the only time you see men wearing black suits around here is for a funeral."

"If you do spot them, can you detain them?"

"They may be violating our summer dress code of t-shirt, shorts, and sandals but that isn't a criminal offense, and I can't arrest someone based on what Alf the bartender overheard them saying. Not that Alf would ever agree to go on the record as to what he overheard since it would be the end of his business if his customers found out. Bartenders are like priests listening to someone confess their sins. Except the only absolution they give is alcoholic."

"You mean he'd take the Fifth," Dick replied, opening a rear door of the unmarked police car and then giving Watson's rump a shove so he could get on the seat.

Sally paused before climbing into the driver's seat and said, "He'd not only take the Fifth, he'd pour the fifth."

CHAPTER ELEVEN

Dick didn't see any men in black lurking around outside the inn when Sally dropped him off. Neither did Watson, or, if he did, he kept it to himself. Dora was standing behind the front desk when Dick and Watson entered. She looked up and said, "Hi, dear. Did you make any progress on finding out who murdered Reverend Wig ... Wiggle ..." Dora paused and then continued, "Oh, you know who I mean."

"Yes, I know who you mean, but no, I haven't solved the case yet. However, Watson and I did find out that there are two men in town who might be up to no good."

Dora closed the book she was reading, *New Faces for Old Places: Marketing Your Historic Inn to Those Who Hate History.* "That's too bad, but you've got enough to do that involves the inn so you shouldn't get waylaid."

"I wasn't waylaid because the no good they're up to involves our inn. The bartender at the High and Dry called me and told me he overheard two customers saying they were going to do some not so nice things to a person staying here."

"I know, because I spoke to the same man. He said he was calling from a bar so I thought he'd just had too much to drink and gave him your number."

"Sally and I think the threat might be real."

"Who's Sally?"

"You know Sally Gilmore the police chief. She said you and she had met."

"I forgot her first name because I was so impressed that the town had a woman police chief."

"Anyway, I was talking to her at the police department when I got the call from Alf, which is the bartender's name."

"Since Sally has to be twice as smart as any male who would have been hired as police chief she shouldn't need your help in catching these guys that Alf overheard."

Deciding it was best not to point out that he wasn't just any male, Dick said, "At this very moment Sally is driving around town to see if she can spot them. It shouldn't be too difficult since two men wearing black suits will certainly stand out."

"That's what I told the two men who checked in."

"What?"

"I mentioned to these two men who were wearing black suits that they certainly stood out since we didn't see many people in that attire here, especially in the summer."

"Was one tall and the other short?"

"Yes, but it was the black suits that seemed out of the ordinary not the difference in their height. Of course, they had a perfectly good explanation. At least it seemed so at the time."

"They did?"

"They said that they were undertakers from Seattle, and they were here to scout sites for destination funerals."

"Destination funerals?"

Dora nodded. "The men explained that they were like destination weddings except people get buried instead of married. They thought our inn would be a perfect venue since it looks more like a church than an inn. In fact, they said it looked more like a church than a lot of churches, especially the new mega churches that look like big box discount stores. I have to agree. I mean, who would want to have a funeral in a Walmart or Costco?"

You can't discount a discount, Dora, Dick wanted to say, but instead asked, "And you believed this story of theirs?"

"Well," Dora said opening the book on her desk, "as it happens, just before they came in, I was reading in this book that destination events like weddings and reunions are something that quaint, historic inns like ours should pursue." She flipped through the pages, stopped, and turned the book to Dick.

Dick leafed quickly through the chapter. "I don't see anything about funerals in here."

Dora turned a page and pointed at a photo of a sculpted vase on top of an alabaster pedestal surrounded by a manicured lawn in front of a New England country inn. "This could be a photo of an urn with someone's ashes in it."

"It seems more likely that you put flowers in it," Dick replied. "Besides an urn with ashes isn't the same thing as a casket with a body in it."

"Yes, but since we could host an actual funeral with a body in a casket, it would give us a marketing advantage."

"We could bury them, so to speak."

"We wouldn't actually bury the deceased person."

"I meant the competition."

Dora's eyes lit up, "However, now that I think about it it, we could offer to scatter their ashes at sea. They do call this area the Graveyard of the Pacific. We could use one of the charter fishing boats in the port. Maybe that Captain you told me about would be interested?"

"I suppose Captain Morgan might be open to the idea, but I suggest we deep six it for now," he said, closing the book and sliding it toward Dora. "However, I see why you believed the story from these guys in black suits that they were a couple of undertakers. But where are they now?"

"They're probably in their room."

"In their room?"

"They said they needed to stay for the night to know what it would be like for the loved ones of the dearly departed who would be staying here."

"I don't understand how you were able to rent them a room if we don't have any vacancies?"

Dora clasped both of her hands on top of the book and said, "Well, it just so happens that the Eidolonic Society has completed their measurements in the room where Elspeth fainted, so that room is now vacant."

"If you don't count the ghost."

"We won't know for certain that there is a ghost until Mr. Thistlewaite gives us the results of their analysis. Even if there is, I thought that since the two men claimed they were undertakers, they wouldn't mind staying in a room that might be haunted. I did tell them it only had one bed, but the short man said that the tall one had a bad back and needed to sleep on something firm so the floor would be perfect. Of course, if I'd known that they were the same people who were in the bar and were up to no good, I never would have rented the room to them." Dora gave a slight smile. "Although I have to admit that if they hadn't brought it up, I probably never would have thought of the inn as a venue for destination funerals. Maybe even men in black suits who are up to no good have good ideas."

"I think a good idea is for me to check in on our new guests."

"You can't just knock on their door and ask them whether they're up to no good," Dora said with alarm. "Who knows how they will respond?"

Annoyed that Dora would think he'd be so stupid, Dick answered, "Watson will be with me."

Dora looked over the counter at Watson, who was snoring at Dick's feet. "I don't think Watson is enough to keep these men at bay."

"All right, I'll take Martin with me, and don't worry, I'll find out what they're up to without them suspecting a thing."

"Martin has the afternoon off. That's why I'm here on the desk." She paused to think for a minute then said. "You should take Lars. Since he's our handyman you can say that you think there might be a problem with the plumbing. Lars can go into the bathroom and jiggle the toilet handle and turn the faucets on and off and tighten something or other with that wrench he carries on his tool belt. That wrench could also come in handy if they get suspicious and you need to subdue them. In fact, why don't you take a wrench as well?"

"I can guarantee they'll be suspicious if they see me with a wrench," Dick said, then patted Dora's hand. "Don't worry, dear, they won't have a clue that I'm gathering clues. Remember I wrote that article 'How Innocent Questions can Elicit Guilty Answers' for the *International Journal of Criminal Interrogations.*"

"How could I forget, honey, since I proofread it for you," Dora replied.

***

Dick turned to Lars, who was standing behind him. "Remember, let me do all the talking. You just go in the bathroom and pretend to check for leaks. You have your wrench, right?"

Lars reached to his tool belt, unholstered the wrench that was dangling next to a hammer and held it up for Dick to see. Dick knocked on the door and announced loudly that it was management coming to check on a possible leak. No one answered so he knocked again and repeated his announcement even louder. When there was still no answer, he put his ear to the door then turned to Lars. "Doesn't seem that they're in their room." He pulled the passkey from his pocket and inserted it into the lock, turned it and opened the door slowly. "Anyone in? We're here about a possible plumbing leak."

After waiting a moment, he walked into the room, Watson trailing him. Dick looked into the bathroom, then turned to Lars who was still standing in the doorway, gripping the wrench in his right hand. "You can come in, Lars. Just in case they come back while we're here, you should go in the bathroom and act like you're looking for a leak."

"I'm not a very good actor," Lars answered.

"Okay, then look for an actual leak. Who knows, maybe you'll find one."

"Right," Lars said, and quickly walked to the bathroom.

Dick searched the room. It wasn't difficult to avoid disturbing anything since there was nothing there. There were no suitcases, the dresser drawers were empty, and there was nothing in the closet but a couple of hangers. He stood there scratching his head as Watson sniffed around.

"Find what you're looking for?" Lars asked from the bathroom door.

"I don't know exactly what I'm looking for, but I know I haven't found it, because there's nothing here to find. Was there anything in the bathroom?"

"Nope, not even a toothbrush." Lars looked dejected, then his face brightened up. "But the good news is there aren't any leaks."

Dick put his hands on his hips and surveyed the room again, "Why don't you take Watson while I lock up the room."

"Watson isn't here."

Dick turned and looked around the room. "Where would he have gone?"

"Look," Lars said. "The cushion of the love seat under the window is on the floor and the access panel for the utility space is open."

"It wasn't like that a minute ago," Dick said walking over to where Lars stood looking into the opening. "Watson must have pulled it off while we were searching the room."

"Why would he do that?"

"He probably thought he was helping me search the room," Dick replied. "You know the saying 'Leave no stone unturned'? Well for Watson, it means no cushion unturned. Obviously, he uncovered a clue, and, being a bloodhound, he's in hot pursuit."

CHAPTER TWELVE

Dick felt as if he'd fallen down a rabbit hole, only it was through a window seat that was also an access hatch for the utility space between the walls, and he was following the tool belt strapped to Lars' backside rather than the fuzzy tail of the Mad Hatter. As unaccustomed as he was not to be taking the lead, Dick had deferred to Lars since he not only had a flashlight, he was also wielding a wrench. After crawling several feet the space allowed them enough headroom to stand up. He whispered, "Where do you think we are now?"

"In the utility space between the walls," Lars whispered back. "Where they put the plumbing lines when they renovated the old church into this inn."

"I know that, Lars," Dick replied sharply. "What I don't know is exactly where we are in this utility space."

"Right. Where are we exactly in this dead utility space?" Lars repeated Dick's question.

"You mean you don't know?"

"Hey, man, I mean Dick, I just started working here, and this is my first time in this utility space," he waved his flashlight around, illuminating pipes. "I feel like one of those peehunkers in a cave."

"You mean spelunker," Dick said. "But it is a bit like a cave. In any case, I guess it isn't important to know exactly where we are, as long as we're still following Watson."

Lars hitched up his tool belt that had been sagging. "And you think Watson is tracking some clue? I mean he could be chasing a raccoon or squirrel that got in here."

Dick shook his head at Lars' suggestion. "Watson is a highly trained bloodhound so he wouldn't go off chasing a raccoon or squirrel. No, he must have picked up the scent of the two men when he pulled off the cushion, and that's what he's following."

Almost on cue, they heard Watson's bark, followed by the sound of scampering feet. It was closer this time.

"We need to hurry. Watson can't be far ahead," Dick said, impatiently then noticed the passageway was lit up from light streaming through a half-open doorway on their right.

"It must be an access door," Lars pointed. "There are a few rooms that have access doors in their closets instead of under the window seat."

They could hear Watson barking on the other side of the door.

"Watson must have them cornered," Dick said.

"What do we do now?"

"Get your wrench ready and go in. I'm right behind you."

"Here," Lars said handing Dick his wrench. "Why don't you go first instead, and I'll be right behind you."

"Okay, okay," Dick muttered, grabbed the wrench, then squeezed past Lars. He pushed the door fully open and found himself in a large closet with men's and women's clothes on hangers.

"Just like I said, this access door is in one of the guest room closets," Lars whispered over Dicks' shoulder.

Dick pushed some of the clothes aside so that he was able to look through the open closet door into the room. He could see Watson who was growling ferociously. Dick slid past the hanging clothes and crept to the doorway to get a better look.

"I'm right behind you," Lars whispered as he pushed Dick. Dick stumbled into the room, the wrench gripped in his right hand. Watson was facing the two men who were standing with their arms raised, their black suits covered with dust.

"Good work, Watson," Dick said.

"I'll say," a voice answered. Dick turned to face Norm Gamble who stood in his bathrobe with a pistol in his hand. Behind him was Donna in something that would have been more revealing if most of her wasn't hidden behind Norm's hefty body. "If I hadn't heard your dog barking, these guys would have got the jump on us."

"What the heck is going on?" Dick asked.

"These two characters here were trying to rob us, that's what was going on," Norm answered then motioned toward the men with his pistol barrel. "Right?"

"We weren't trying to rob you, mister," the short man in black said. "We just checked into our room and Roscoe here," he prodded the tall man next to him with his shoulder, "he goes over to the bench under the window and when he sits down on the cushion his butt sinks and not because it's some soft cushion. I help him up and we see that there's an opening under the cushion."

"The access hatch. It goes to the utility space inside the wall," Dick said.

"Yeah," the short guy says, nodding his head vigorously. "The access hatch. When Roscoe sat on the cushion there was nothing to stop him sinking into it."

"Is this going anywhere, because I'm not in the mood for storytelling," Norm said, his pistol still trained on the two men.

"Sure, it's going somewhere. See, after I pulled Roscoe's big butt out we hear a cat, right Roscoe?" Roscoe nodded and imitated the sound of a cat's meow. "It sounded something like that," the short man said, then continued. "I'm Max, by the way. Roscoe and I are both cat lovers, so of course we had to save this cat even if it meant our suits would get dirty, which you can see, they are. Anyway, I take out my cellphone and turn on its flashlight and Roscoe and I crawl inside. We're in this passageway back there trying to find the cat when we hear this dog barking behind us. We figure it must be chasing the cat.

That's when I see a door so I open it and there's this closet, the one you just came out of, and we can hear this dog is getting pretty close, so we run inside the closet and open the door and find out we're in this room, and then here you are with a gun pointing at us. It's as simple as that."

"Simple?" Norm grunted. "You must think I'm a simpleton to believe that the reason you break into my room is because you were just trying to find a lost cat."

"I swear it's the truth, ain't it Roscoe?" Max turned to Roscoe.

Roscoe nodded in agreement, "Everything except the part about my butt being big."

Without lowering his pistol, Norm turned to Dick, "Are these characters really staying here?"

"They just checked in," Dick said, glumly.

"They're right about the access hatch, but we didn't hear any cat," Lars added.

"Well, who was the dog chasing after if it wasn't a cat?" Max asked.

"You two." Dick offered.

"Why would he be chasing us?" Roscoe asked.

"Because you were supposed to be in the room and you weren't, and the access hatch was open, and if there had been a cat, Watson would still be chasing it."

"And you guys are both wearing black suits," Lars added.

"Yeah," Norm said. "What's with the black suits?"

"They claim they're undertakers," Dick said.

"We prefer funeral directors," Max said.

"Well, I prefer you two to get the hell out of here," Norm said.

"Shouldn't we call the police?" Donna said over Norm's shoulder.

"Nah, these guys know what's what." Norm waved the pistol toward the door and said, "Now get out, and if I see your sorry faces again, you'll be directing your own funerals." The men started moving toward the door, their arms still raised. "And you can give Chuck the same message."

"We don't know anyone named Chuck," Max said.

"Tell him anyway," Norm grunted. "Now scram before I change my mind and decide to press charges for home invasion..."

"It's not your home, it's a hotel room," Max said.

"An historic inn not a hotel," Dick corrected him.

"Whatever the hell it is, you're invading it, so get lost," Norm growled, waving the pistol barrel in the direction of the door.

The two men in black backed out of the room with their hands still up in the air and then quickly disappeared down the hall. Norm turned to Dick and said, "What kind of place are you running here? First there's people keeping us awake by walking back and forth in that hidden passageway..."

"Not people, but ghosts," Donna said.

"Utility space, and it was squirrels or a raccoon, not a ghost," Dick said.

"Whatever it was, it kept us awake. And then these two jerks pop out of the closet and claim they're trying to rescue a cat."

"It won't happen again. We're going to make sure that there's nothing in the utility space, be they squirrels, raccoons, or cats or whatever. Lars will put a lock on that access door in the closet."

"But that won't keep any ghosts out," Donna said. "They can walk through walls."

"Enough with the ghosts, honey," Norm said over his shoulder then turned back to Dick. "Give us a few minutes to dress before you put a lock on the door." After Donna whispered in his ear he added, "Make that an hour."

"If you don't mind my asking, do you usually travel with a gun?" Dick asked in a matter-of-fact voice.

Norm lowered the pistol. "Hey, I've got a permit to carry it to protect myself, and especially my bride from people like those two jerks."

"And from any ghosts who might walk through the walls," Donna added.

"No, honey, you need silver bullets for ghosts."

"For werewolves," Dick said.

"You have werewolves here as well?" Donna gasped.

"No, I mean silver bullets are used to kill werewolves, not ghosts, but there aren't any werewolves here, and if there are any ghosts who might happen to walk through the walls, they're friendly."

"And they won't mess with your clothes, because they only wear sheets," Lars added.

"See, there's nothing to worry about, babe," Norm said. In response Donna put her arms around him and planted a big kiss on his cheek. He turned to Dick and Lars and said, "Shut the door on your way out."

Dick followed Lars out of the room with Watson at his heels. Just beyond the doorway he turned and asked Norm, "Just who is this Chuck that you mentioned?"

"Chuck's just a guy I did some business with who thinks he got the short end. He's not just a real loser, but a sore one. I wouldn't put it past him to hire those two guys who claim they're undertakers to try and shake me down."

"What kind of business was it?" Dick asked.

"The none of your business kind," Norm growled, then closed the door in Dick's face.

CHAPTER THIRTEEN

After Dick told Dora about finding the men in black inside the Gambles' room, Dora's response was that it sounded like a game of cat and mouse only the mice were chasing the cat and Dick and Lars were chasing the mice.

"More like two rats than mice," Dick replied.

"We don't know they were rats, Dick. They might really be funeral directors like they claim, and they did have an explanation or an alibi, as you would say, when they said they were trying to rescue a cat."

"A highly improbable alibi."

"But not impossible, and you're the person who's so fond of quoting Sherlock Holmes as saying that when you eliminate the impossible, whatever remains, however improbable, must be the truth," Dora said with a fleeting wink of her eye.

Dora was right about his fondness for the quote, and it had come back to haunt him. Dick sighed, "Alright, I won't eliminate ghosts and cats or, even, a ghost cat, but I'll keep an eye on the men in black just the same."

"You'll have to find them first, because they just checked out. They said that they had a sudden change of plans," Dora replied with a smile. She had won, but didn't have to rub it in. After all, unless you wanted your marriage to turn into a war between the spouses, one should be gracious in victory, which was always better than having to be the good loser.

"After Norm Gamble drew his gun on them, I don't think they will try breaking in again."

"A gun?"

"He has a permit so he's allowed to carry it," Dick said. "I suppose he might sue us if we asked him to leave."

"Not might, he would sue us, and he'd win."

"Excuse me," Terry Tarantella interrupted. "But have you seen my daughter?"

"No," Dora answered.

"I don't understand. She was supposed to wait here for me. We're going to go to the beach and she didn't want to wait in our room while I decided what to wear. She considers choosing what to wear a waste of time, which is why she only wears sweatpants and a hoodie."

"I love your sundress, by the way," Dora said.

"Oh this," Terry said, obviously flattered. "I just bought it for the trip. I'm wearing my swimsuit under it. One piece - my bikini days are behind me. Don't worry I'm not going to swim with all those riptides and whatever you warned us about. I just plan on lying on a beach towel and doing some wading in the water. Natalya, on the other hand, who doesn't have a bit of cellulite, doesn't want the sun to ruin her skin's perfect shade of pale, so she'll be fully covered in her sweatpants and a black hoodie sitting under a beach umbrella that I brought with us." Terry looked around. "You're sure you haven't seen her."

"No, but we were distracted with a little business meeting so she could have walked by without us noticing her."

"Maybe she's waiting for you outside ... in the shade," Dick offered.

"Yes, that's probably where she is. I'll just go look," Terry answered, then picked up her canvas bag and walked out the front door. A couple of minutes later she returned and said with alarm. "She's not out there. It's like she just disappeared."

"What about trying her cellphone," Dora suggested.

Terry winced and said, "I made her leave it in the room. I told her she needed to experience the ocean, the waves crashing on the beach instead of looking at a tiny screen."

"It's actually a calm day so there probably won't be much crashing of waves on the beach," Dora noted.

"More of a lapping, which is quite soothing," Dick said.

Terry shrugged. "She wasn't happy about not having her phone, but then I told her that we could go horseback riding afterwards, and that there were probably no bars on the beach anyway."

Dick was about to point out that Natalya was underage and couldn't be served even if there were bars when Dora saved him from embarrassment by saying. "Yes, the cell service on the beach is pretty spotty at best."

"Not to mention the damage salt air and sand can inflict on digital devices," Dick added.

"I just hope she isn't so mad at me that she's run away again."

"Again?" Dick asked.

"Yes, she has a bad habit of running away when she gets angry with me," Terry replied. "Usually, she just goes to the local coffee shop and has one of those mocha drinks and looks at her cellphone."

"The Grist and Grind down at the port is the only coffee shop that isn't a drive thru," Dora said.

"She doesn't have a driver's license, not that it would stop her if she was really mad, but our car is still out front and I have the keys."

"Why don't we take my car and drive down to the Grist and Grind?" Dora suggested.

"She's not a fast walker so we might even see her on the way there," Terry added, her face brightened with hope.

"While we're gone, Dick can look for her around here. There are lots of places to hide in the inn," Dora said then looked at Dick. "In fact, Dick was just telling me about one he had discovered."

After Dora and Terry left, Dick woke up Watson who was taking a nap on the rug next to the front desk. "Nap time is over, Watson, we need to find someone else dressed in black, but with a hood."

"Have you seen Natalya?" Dick asked Martha Digby, who was standing at the bottom of the stairway. "She's a teenage girl wearing sweatpants and a black hoodie. Her mother is looking for her."

"I was just on my way to the front desk to ask if you'd seen Trevor," she responded. "He went out with his skateboard and was supposed to be back by now. We're going to the beach to fly the kite that we bought. Trevor and Gerald even watched a YouTube together on how to fly a kite."

"Do you think Trevor and Natalya could be together?" Dick asked.

Martha thought for a moment before answering, "They were talking with each other at breakfast. It was more like sharing each other's cellphone screens than talking. I guess they could have met up, but where would they go?"

"Apparently Natalya has a habit of running away to coffee shops and the only one in town is Grist and Grind at the port. My wife and Terry, Natalya's mom, are on their way down there. I'll text her and tell her to be on the lookout for Trevor as well. In the meantime, Watson and I will add Trevor to our search list in the inn."

"What can my husband and I do?"

"You could look around outside. They might be somewhere on the grounds."

After Martha walked off to get her husband, Dick and Watson started their search. "Now where would a teenage girl and boy go if they were together? Assuming they are together, which is more probable than not," he muttered to Watson. "Since neither Natalya nor Trevor has a driver's license ..." Dick walked over to one of the front windows and looked out. "And, in any case, their parents' cars are still parked outside, so we can eliminate that they went for a drive and parked somewhere to look at the view and maybe, well, you know." He looked at Watson and added. "No, you probably don't." Watson answered with a bark and then ran through the parlor and stopped in front of the door to the former sanctuary.

Dick opened the door and walked in. Through the dim light he could make out two figures sitting on the floor of the raised platform at the front, which was where the pulpit and communion table had been when the inn was a church, but had since been converted into a stage. Their legs were crossed and they were looking down at something. Dick followed Watson who ran up the steps to one side of the stage. Natalya and Trevor looked up, startled. "Hey, you two," Dick called out as he walked toward them. "Do you know your parents are looking for you?"

Both Natalya and Trevor looked up at Dick. Natalya said, "We're talking to a ghost."

"What?" Dick stammered and looked down. Both of their hands were on a small heart shaped piece of wood on top of a board with large block letters printed on it as well as the words 'Yes' and 'No' and the numbers 0 through 9. "Where did you get that Ouija board?"

"I found it in that room you call a parlor the other night when the bells woke us up," Natalya answered. "They said it might be ghosts that rang them, so I asked Trevor if he'd help me contact them. I was too scared to do it by myself."

"I play Zombie Apocalypse all the time, so it's really not scary even though these are ghosts not zombies," Trevor said with more than a little teenager bravado.

"We'd rather do this than the dumb things our parents want," Natalya said, firmly.

"Dumb or not, your parents are worried sick and looking all over for you," Dick said. "Now quit what you're doing and give me the Ouija board."

The heart shaped piece of wood that both Natalya and Trevor's hands were on moved suddenly across the board until it stopped on the word 'No.'

"Look," Trevor said. "He doesn't want us to stop."

"Who doesn't want you to stop?" Dick said, exasperated.

"The ghost, who else?" Natalya said, as if it wasn't perfectly clear.

"There aren't any ghosts," Dick said. "That's just the power of suggestion that's made your hands move the piece on the board to 'No'."

"What about the bells that rang last night?"

Dick sighed. "Like I said at the time, it was a recording of bells ringing, played over the old PA speakers in the steeple that we heard, not ghosts."

"But what if you're wrong and it really was a ghost?"

"A ghost could have played the recording," Trevor chimed in.

"I know!" Natalya said. "Why don't we ask him if he ever rang the bells?" Before Dick could respond, the piece in their hands started to move across the board and stopped on the word 'Yes.'

"Wow!" exclaimed Trevor. "This is better than Zombie Apocalypse."

"Look, we don't have time for any more games, now give me the Ouija board and we'll all go to the front desk and wait for your parents."

They reluctantly took their hands off the piece of wood, then Natalya folded the board and placed it in a box along with the heart shaped piece. She handed the box to Dick who put it under his right arm. "Now get up and follow me."

"Okay," Natalya said. "But the Captain is going to be really pissed that you stopped us."

Dick stopped and asked, wearily, "What captain are you talking about?"

"The ghost, of course," she answered giving him a how dumb can you be look. "He told us that we should call him Captain."

CHAPTER FOURTEEN

Dick ordered Natalya and Trevor to wait in the parlor where he could keep an eye on them until their parents returned. He had to admit that he was a little thrown when they said they had been talking to a ghost addressed as Captain. Then the obvious explanation came to him – they must have overheard Martin talking about Captain Johnson at the cocktail hour. Yes, that was it, Dick thought. Then bending down and cradling the Ouija board, he whispered to Watson, "Leave it to overactive teenage imaginations to think they were communicating with a ghost on this Ouija board." Watson sniffed at the board and then ran in the opposite direction, darting behind the couch where Natalya and Trevor were sitting.

"See, he's scared because he smelled the ghost we were talking to," Natalya smirked.

"Yeah, dead people really stink," Trevor added. "At least zombies do."

Deciding that arguing with teenagers was as useless as trying to cajole Watson out from behind the couch, Dick shrugged, pulled out his cellphone, and called Dora. After telling her that he'd found Natalya and Trevor and that she and Terry could come back to the inn, he walked over to Martin who had returned and taken up his position behind the front desk. Placing the Ouija board on the desk, he explained how Natalya and Trevor had disappeared and he had found them playing with the Ouija board. "They said they found it on a shelf in the parlor. I'm no expert on Ouija boards, but it looks pretty old."

"Indeed, it is," Martin replied. "If you look on the back you'll see that it was manufactured in 1875."

"Really?" Dick answered, taking the board and looking at it himself. He put it down and said, "Now that's a real antique. How did it end up in our parlor?"

"They found it when they were renovating the old church into the inn."

"I haven't spent a lot of time in churches, but I'm pretty sure that a Ouija board isn't something that goes with hymnals and Bibles, so I wonder how it got there."

"Yes, I can see what you mean," Martin replied, stroking his chin. "Anyway, I was told that a workman found it and gave it to Mr. McTavish who must have put the Ouija board in the parlor along with the other antiques he'd collected. I don't recall anyone ever playing with it, although playing is probably the wrong word for ... well ..." Martin stammered.

"Communicating with ghosts?" Dick suggested.

"Yes, but, of course, I don't believe in that sort of thing, although some people do."

"Obviously, or there wouldn't be Ouija boards ..."

"Ouija boards!" a voice boomed from behind him.

Dick answered without turning around, "Oh, some of the kids found this old Ouija board in the parlor and we were just discussing what a lot of nonsense it is that you can communicate with the dead."

Turning around he saw that the voice belonged to Cedric Thistlewaite, and he hastily added, "using a Ouija board."

"You're quite correct that a Ouija board is hardly a scientific apparatus for paranormal communication," Cedric replied looking more closely at the board. "I would guess that this one is at least a hundred years old."

"It was manufactured in 1875," Martin said.

"I must say it is remarkably well-preserved despite its age."

"Still in working order according to the kids who were playing around with it," Dick said.

"One shouldn't play around with a Ouija board. Although they aren't a device that a scientist would use, there are documented cases of them being employed successfully to contact the other side. Of course, it requires someone with skill and discernment to use them properly otherwise ... well ..."

"Otherwise, what?" Martin asked, leaning over the front desk.

"I'll just reiterate that a Ouija board is not a game. It should especially be kept out of the reach of those who lack the requisite maturity to understand what is real as opposed to what is imagined," Cedric rolled his eyes toward Trevor and Natalya and added, "if you get my drift?"

"You're saying that they should be kept out of the hands of young people?"

"I heard you," Natalya shouted from the couch. "You may think we're stupid, but we have better hearing than you old people."

Dick turned to Natalya and Trevor and said, "Mr. Thistle-waite didn't say that you were stupid."

"He was just pointing out that a Ouija board isn't appropriate for impressionable minds who might imagine they were communicating with a ghost," Martin added in a soothing voice.

"We didn't imagine it," Trevor blurted out. "The Captain was really talking to us."

"Captain?" Cedric asked, barely hiding his annoyance.

"That's the name we got when we asked who we were speaking with," Trevor answered. "I heard that a lot of ships sank around here, so there must be a lot of ghosts who were captains."

"Why would a captain who went down with his ship want to talk to two kids?" Cedric asked skeptically.

"Because he thought we were looking for the buried treasure," Natalya answered.

"Buried treasure," Cedric said. "It sounds like you've been watching that movie Pirates of the Something or Other."

"*Pirates of the Caribbean*," Trevor answered. "I've watched all five of them, but the first one is still the best."

"What else did this captain say?"

"Nothing. Mr. Carlson stopped us before we had a chance to ask."

"Now we'll never know where the treasure is buried," Natalya said crossing her arms and pouting.

Before Dick could answer, Dora walked through the front door, followed by Terry and the Digbys. As the families reunited in the parlor, Dora joined Dick and the others at the front desk. "What's this buried treasure that Natalya was talking about when we walked in?" she asked.

Dick explained how he had discovered Natalya and Trevor with an old Ouija board and that they thought they had contacted a ghost.

"Who was the ghost?"

"Mr. Carlson interrupted them before they could find out," Martin answered.

"Finding Natalya and Trevor and returning them to their parents was the priority, not letting them play with a Ouija board," Dick explained.

Dora patted Dick on the arm. "Of course, dear. How did they ever get a hold of a Ouija board, anyway?"

"It was in your parlor of all places," Cedric said accusingly. "And as I told your husband in no uncertain terms, it should not be in a place where just anyone can get their hands on it. It isn't a game and certainly not something that children should be playing with."

"You're saying that we should lock it up in a safe rather than have it on a shelf?" Dick asked.

Ignoring Dick, Dora asked Cedric, "You really think that's necessary?"

"Although Ouija boards aren't something we use in our scientific investigations of paranormal activity, there is some evidence that they might provide a crude form of communication with the spirit world."

"A friend of mine said they've used an online Ouija board," Martin piped up.

"Those are scams. The spirit world isn't accessible online. It's not like you can friend them on Facebook."

"From what I've heard being dead doesn't seem to unfriend a person on Facebook," Dora pointed out.

"Like being ghosted in reverse by the digitally undead," Dick added.

"You think it's funny, but as a scientist I can tell you that playing with the spirit world is no laughing matter," Cedric said. "As we like to say, ghosts should be taken with deadly seriousness." He picked up the Ouija board and looked at it closely, "I must say, it is in pristine condition considering how old it is. You know, it would make a fine addition to our historical archives."

"You mean you want to buy it?" Dora asked. "How much are you willing to pay?"

"Pay?" Cedric replied. "I was thinking more on the lines of a donation. The Eidolonic Society is a nonprofit, so you would get a charitable tax deduction."

"Maybe we should do some research first. It might be worth quite a lot,"

"I doubt it," Cedric said dismissively. "There really aren't many people who collect Ouija boards."

Dick took the Ouija board from Cedric. "Before we decide what we want to do with it, I'd like to show it to someone and get his opinion."

Cedric's right eyebrow arched as he asked, "And who would this someone be?"

"As a matter of fact, he's a captain. Only he's still alive."

CHAPTER FIFTEEN

As they sat on the deck of the Hard to Fathom, Morgan Murray ran the fingers of his right hand through his unruly beard and listened intently to Dick's account of finding Natalya and Trevor with the Ouija board. Dick handed the board to Morgan, who examined it and said, "Well, now, that sure makes sense."

"What makes sense?" Dick asked.

"Why look right here and you can see the initials B.W.," Morgan replied holding up the board and pointing at the initials.

Dick looked closely and asked, "Whose initials are they?"

"They have to be Beau Wheelock's. He was a medium who held séances that were organized by his aunt, Betty Wheelock. She was a big believer in spiritualism."

"Okay, so?"

"So the Wheelocks bought Captain Johnson's property from his estate. Right after they bought it, Betty held a séance in the house with her nephew, Beau, as the medium. They were trying to conjure up the ghost of Captain Johnson to ask him to reveal where the treasure was hidden."

"What happened?"

"From the eyewitness account I've read, the Captain's ghost made an appearance, but instead of telling them where he hid his fortune, he told them to get the hell out of his house. It wasn't a voice, of course, it was spelled out on the Ouija board. Must have been this very one."

Morgan tapped the board. "Apparently it was a captain's order that they couldn't refuse, because shortly after the séance the Wheelocks sold the house and surrounding land to the organizers of the new church."

"The land where the inn is now," Dick said, gravely nodding his head. "How reliable is this eyewitness account?"

"The account is straight out of Betty Wheelock's diary, which is now in the History Society's archives. I don't know why she would write in her diary something she made up since it was supposed to be private. Not that I'm saying it was really the ghost of Captain Johnson rather than some trick of Beau's. Still, if it were Beau, not the ghost of Captain Johnson, why would he want to stop a séance from continuing? And, not only that, to stop any further séances since that was his business."

"But if it wasn't Beau pretending to be Captain Johnson's ghost then who made the planchette move?"

"Aye," Morgan sighed and handed the Ouija board back to Dick. "I'd say that's a mystery."

Dick cradled the board in his hands and said, "And another mystery is how this Ouija board ended up in the inn's parlor."

"If only it could speak," Morgan laughed heartily, his broad shoulders shaking.

***

"Well, now," Martin said, looking at the Ouija board after Dick had placed it on the front desk and told him and Dora what Morgan had said. "As I told you before, all I know is that the workmen who converted the church to the inn found it and gave it to Mr. McTavish, so he must have put it in the parlor."

"Then Farley McTavish must know all about it," Dora said.

"Do you have his phone number?" Dick asked.

Dora quickly recited the number and added, "I know it by heart because of all the questions I've had after we bought the inn, although he doesn't answer his phone very often. Usually I have to leave a message when I call and he gets back to me ... eventually. We'd have better luck seeing him in person."

"Give me his address and I'll put it into my map app," Dick said, taking out his cellphone.

Dora put her hand over his phone and said, "Speaking from personal experience, dear, you'll have to resort to the old-fashioned way of getting there."

"And what way is that, honey?"

"Using a right seat navigator who knows the way, which in this case is me."

Ten minutes later Dora provided directions as they drove out of Ilwaco on Pacific Highway past the hospital and Black Lake and into Seaview. Dora called it a beach town, although it was barely a village in Dick's estimation and he couldn't see the beach. They took a left down a narrow lane past small, one-story mid-twentieth century houses that Dora called beach bungalows. After a couple of blocks, the street came to a dead end but Dora told Dick to keep driving.

"Where?" Dick replied. "All I see is a path through the trees."

"That's not a path, it's his driveway."

"If that's his driveway, and I think calling it that is a stretch, where's his house?"

"You can't see it from here. It's a very long driveway," Dora replied. "Now you can see why you need me to navigate."

They slowly drove up the driveway, the branches and wind-stunted spruce and lodgepole pines brushing the sides of the car, until they reached a clearing where they saw a two-story house with a peaked roof and a widow's walk perched on top. The house faced the Pacific Ocean, although the beach was hidden by dunes covered with seagrass. As soon as they stepped out of the car, they were met by the sound of the surf and the smell of salt water. They followed a stone path that led around to the west side of the house where a broad veranda faced the ocean.

As they approached the steps to the veranda, Farley Mc-Tavish appeared. He was a short, energetic-looking man with a ruddy complexion and grey hair peeking out from under a blue baseball cap with 'IF YOU FOUND ME YOU'RE LOST' stenciled on it. "When I heard the car I thought it was another tourist who'd gotten lost," he said as he took off the hat. "What a pleasant surprise to see it's you, Dora."

Dora introduced Dick, and Farley invited them to have a seat in one of the half dozen Adirondack chairs. After they were seated, Farley asked, "Is this a social visit or something about the inn?"

'Both," Dora answered. "We thought you might shed some light on a little mystery."

"Oh," Farley replied rubbing his hands together. "I love a good mystery unless it involves plumbing. I never did understand the plumbing at the inn so I'm afraid I won't be much help if that's what it involves."

"This involves the Ouija board in the parlor," Dick said.

"In the parlor, you say?"

"Some kids whose families are staying at the inn found a Ouija board on a shelf," Dora added. "When we asked Martin about it, he said you would know how it got there."

Farley stroked his stubble chin and said, "A workman came across it when we were renovating the church into an inn. It was an antique and in mint condition." He chuckled, "I'd say it was still in working condition if I believed in that mumbo jumbo."

Dick said, "I spoke with Morgan Murray about it, and he thinks it belonged to Beau Wheelock who held a séance in Captain Johnson's house before it mysteriously burned down."

"Morgan should know. He's quite the expert on local history."

"Any idea how it ended up in the church?" Dick pressed.

"Well, I hardly think the church would have wanted a Ouija board around, so it must have been left there by someone else after the church was closed. The building was empty until I bought it and converted it into the inn. I think some folks must have broken into the place and used the Quija board for a séance to see if they could conjure up the ghost of old Captain Johnson and ask him where he buried his treasure."

"You believe this story about Captain Johnson burying a treasure somewhere on the property?" Dora asked.

Farley shrugged and held both of his hands up. "What I will say is that it wasn't bad for business. People love a mystery, right?"

"Some more than others," Dora replied, shooting Dick a look.

Farley chuckled. "As long as no one tore up the floorboards or dug holes on the property, there was no harm in it that I could see."

"But why would these people leave the Ouija board behind after the séance?" Dick asked.

Farley shrugged and replied, "Maybe they had to leave in a hurry and ditched it."

"You think someone caught them trespassing?" Dora asked.

Farley smiled and replied, "Either that or..."

"Or?"

"Captain Johnson's ghost appeared and scared the bejesus out of them," Farley said and then laughed heartily. "Not that I believe that supernatural mumbo jumbo, as I said, but anyone who would play with a Ouija board is susceptible to seeing things that aren't there. Like those kids you mentioned."

Dora nodded and said, "In other words these trespassers brought the Ouija board there and left it behind, then a worker found it during the renovation and gave it to you," Dora said and turned to Dick. "I guess that solves our mystery, honey." She pushed on the broad arms of her chair to get up. "We're sorry to bother you with such a silly thing, Farley."

"No need to apologize," Farley said, almost leaping from his chair in a display of near gymnastic agility.

After Dick stood up he said, "It does seem like quite a coincidence that the Ouija board these trespassers used once belonged to Beau Wheelock."

"Oh Dick," Dora replied. "The simple explanation is that they bought it at some antique store. Everything doesn't have to be a mystery."

"Yes, I suppose you're right, dear," Dick answered, his voice tinged with disappointment.

Farley scratched his chin and said, "Still, there is one mystery that remains."

"What's that?" Dick asked, eagerly.

"How the Ouija board ended up in the parlor. I don't remember putting it there since it didn't fit with the nautical theme. I recall locking it in a trunk in the storage room. Then

Martin told me he found it in the parlor and asked about it. I told him the story about finding it, but left out that I didn't remember putting it there."

CHAPTER SIXTEEN

"I'm beginning to think that there really might be something mysterious going on," Dora told Dick after they were back in their car.

Steering the car slowly out the long drive Dick resisted the urge to respond with, "It's about time," and wisely replied, "Why don't we stop at the Station Restaurant and talk about it over dinner and drinks, honey?"

"Why Dick, are you suggesting we have a date night?" Dora answered with more than a little flirtatiousness in her voice.

"More a date late afternoon," Dick replied after quickly checking the time on the dashboard clock and seeing it was only 5 p.m.

Dora patted Dick's thigh with her left hand, "I'll take what I can get."

Dick pulled into one of the empty parking spaces next to the former train station. Usually they were all full, but since the restaurant opened at 5 p.m., there weren't any other cars. "We shouldn't have any trouble getting a table at this hour, even without a reservation," he said.

"I wouldn't bet on it. There are a lot of people around here who are early to bed, early to rise, which means they eat early as well. Still, we promote it to our guests, and I've gotten to know the owners, Marge and Les, so I'm sure they'll accommodate us."

Indeed, they did. As soon as they entered Marge, a middle-aged, bright-eyed woman with a broad smile, greeted Dora like an old friend. Although the restaurant was empty, as Dora had predicted, there were a number of reservations for 5:30 p.m. "But I can seat you at a corner table near the Chef's Window."

"The Chef's Window?" Dick asked.

Marge laughed, "We took out part of the wall separating the kitchen from the dining room so that Les, my husband, who is also the chef, doesn't feel all cooped up. We call it the Chef's Window. The Chef's Table is the one directly below the window and people sitting there can talk with Les as he cooks."

"Sort of like the Captain's Table on a cruise ship," Dick said looking at the far end of the dining room where a man in chef's white waved at them through the open 'window.'

"That's where we got the idea," Marge said. "We went on a cruise after we decided to leave Portland and open a restaurant here. Les said he wanted something like a Captain's Table in the restaurant so that he could interact directly with the customers.

That was the only thing he liked about the cruise. He thought the food was awful, and that was before he got seasick."

"Dick feels the same way. He's a criminologist and we went on a cruise where he and some other experts were part of a program about crime on the high seas."

"I wouldn't have agreed except for ..." Dick nodded his head at Dora. "They had a gala with everyone dressed up as pirates, including the captain."

"Everyone but Dick," Dora said, squeezing his arm playfully. "It was a good thing they weren't real pirates or you would have ended up marooned on a desert island."

"Instead of being marooned on a floating one," Dick said. "But at least since I was a speaker, all of our expenses were covered, so the cruise didn't cost us any pieces of eight."

Settling into the corner table, they ordered drinks from a smiling woman named Emily whom Dora knew from previous visits. After introducing Dick, Dora asked Emily about her family. Emily launched into an update, which was quite lengthy because she lived on a cranberry farm with her husband, two children, her parents, one grandmother, a dog, three cats and a dozen chickens. Finally, Dick interrupted by clearing his throat vigorously and saying it was quite dry.

"I'm sorry, Mr. Carlson, I'll bring you both some water right away," Emily said.

"Could you put some scotch in the water?" Dick asked and then added, "Make that more scotch than water."

"I'll have a gin and tonic with a glass of water on the side," Dora said.

After Emily left to get their drinks, Dora said, "Isn't it refreshing to be in a place where people remember that they've served you before and are genuinely friendly. This is maybe the third time Emily has served me, and I know more about her than I ever did about the waiters in the restaurants we frequented in New York."

"In New York they're all young, single actors working tables while waiting for their big break, so what else is there to know about them? Frankly, the only thing they were interested in knowing about us was how big a tip we would leave."

When Emily returned with their drinks, they asked for some time to enjoy their cocktails before ordering dinner.

"Bells ring in our steeple in the middle of the night, then something scares our maid enough that she faints while cleaning a vacant room, then two men in black, claiming to be undertakers, break into a room through a secret passageway and accost our guests, and then some kids say that a ghost has spoken to them using a Ouija board that they found in our parlor, and we just found out from Farley, the inn's original owner who sold it to us, that some workers found the Ouija board during renovation but he locked it away in storage and doesn't remember taking it out and putting it on the shelf in the parlor." Dora stopped her recitation to sip her gin and tonic, then put the glass down and added, "Have I got all of that straight?"

"More or less," Dick replied, having already taken a couple of swigs of scotch while listening to her.

"Is it more of the more or more of the less?"

"It's just that you skipped over some facts."

"It's only an overview," Dora replied defensively.

"Exactly, dear," Dick said in a conciliatory voice. "And it's a very good overview of the mysterious events that have occurred."

Dora took another drink and leaned over the table toward Dick, "What do you make of it? Are all these mysterious events connected, and if so, who's behind it and what could possibly be their motive?"

"It could just be a series of unconnected incidents," Dick offered, then took another sip of scotch.

"Is that what you think?"

"Not really. One might be a coincidence, but four is a stretch," Dick shook his head. "That's why I need to find out if they are connected and, if so, who's behind it and why?"

"It's not just you, it's we."

"I thought you tasked me with this while you manage the inn?"

"I did, but I changed my mind."

"You don't think I can do it by myself?"

Dora reached out and patted Dick's left hand. "I just think it would be better to do it together. As a team. I realize that you can't have all the fun."

"Isn't managing the inn fun enough? I mean, it's what you wanted to do."

"Oh, Dick," Dora sighed. "It's satisfying, but you know I've always loved mysteries."

"You certainly love your English mystery books. I see that cozy mysteries have replaced the Cussler and other authors you banished from the parlor bookshelf."

"I know you hate them but they're the kind of books that go with a place like ours"

"I just think they're silly, especially Agatha Christie's Miss Marple. I mean, how much crime can there be in a sleepy, English village with its old church and ..." Dick stopped.

"And?" Dora said with a smile as Dick looked into his almost empty glass of scotch.

"Okay, and Ilwaco is a sleepy village and the inn is an old church," Dick answered then drank the rest of his scotch.

Before Dora could say 'gotcha' to Dick, Emily arrived and asked if they were ready to order dinner. They ordered a salad to share and the locally caught salmon as well as two glasses of a Washington State sauvignon blanc. As Emily walked away, Dora whispered to Dick, "Don't turn around, but guess who's coming to dinner?"

"Who?"

"The Gambles."

"Fortunately, we have a table that only seats two," Dick replied, wondering if they might have to amend their drink order to a bottle of sauvignon blanc rather than two glasses. "Maybe they'll put them on the far side of the dining room."

"I'm afraid not. Marge is leading them to this end of the dining room," Dora whispered.

"Maybe they won't notice us," Dick whispered back, regretting that since they had already ordered dinner there were no menus to hide behind.

"Too late, dear, we've been spotted."

Dick turned to his right just in time to see Donna Gamble waving at them. They were standing with Marge who had led them to the Chef's Table. Norm walked over and slapped Dick on the back, "This place must be as good as your man Martin said if the inn's owners are eating here."

"Martin was able to get us a reservation for the Chef's Table, which is supposed to be the best seat in the house," Donna added. "And look at that, it's right next to you two!"

"Hope you don't mind being second best," Norm said with a laugh. "This is pretty early for us. We're nightbirds back in Seattle, but we haven't been getting that much sleep since we got here."

Dora said, "I'm sorry about the bells in the middle of the night and then those dreadful men who ..."

"Those two jerks got the message," Norm cut her off. "Anyway, that's not been the only thing keeping us from sleeping," Norm replied with a wink, then put his arm around Donna, "Right, honey?"

Donna blushed and Norm said, "That's the thing with blondes like Donna, they can't hide it when they turn red. I like it just like I like my steak, rare."

"Martin said the steak here is excellent," Donna said as the blush receded from her face.

"I've never tried the steak, but that's what I hear," Dora replied.

"Since we'll be sitting at the Chef's Table it'll be easy to send it back if it's not the way I want it," Norm said.

"We should sit down, Norm," Donna said, "and let these two enjoy their dinner."

"Right," Norm replied, then cracked, "I'm so hungry I could eat a bear, but I guess I'll have to settle for a steak."

After Donna and Norm went to their table Dora leaned forward and whispered, "Norm doesn't seem very concerned about those two men who broke into his room. Didn't you tell me that he said some guy named Chuck sent them, with whom he'd had a falling out over business?"

Dick nodded his head. "That's what he claimed, but he wouldn't say anything more about Chuck or what their dispute was, and he declined to press charges against the two guys who broke in. Maybe because he didn't want to disclose any details about a disagreement that would be serious enough to lead to a break-in. In any case, Norm seemed confident that this Chuck character would get the message and not mess with him anymore."

"Do you think that this Chuck could be behind the other things that happened?"

"The problem with that theory is that if this mysterious Chuck is only interested in Norm, what would be his motive for the other incidents that you provided such a great overview of, like ringing the steeple bells in the middle of the night, scaring a maid who was making up an empty room, and frightening two kids who were playing with a Ouija board?"

"Not to mention that Chuck would need to know about the Ouija board and then move it to the shelf of the parlor."

"And know that Natalya and Trevor would decide to play with it."

"Maybe they're all red herrings," Dora said. "Misleading clues that are intended to put us on the wrong track. Like in an Agatha Christie mystery."

"Agatha has enough red herrings in her books to supply a fish cannery for a year," Dick replied. "But yes, dear, it's possible that some of the incidents are intended to lead us in the wrong direction or…"

"Or what?"

"Whoever hired the two men in black has nothing to do with the other mysterious incidents that have occurred."

"But you said that you didn't believe it was a coincidence."

"I said one might be a coincidence, but four was a stretch. A stretch doesn't mean it's impossible, only improbable."

"We've already talked about what your man Sherlock had to say about the difference between improbable and impossible,"

Dora said with a smile. "But Agatha Christie said that one coincidence is just a coincidence, two coincidences are a clue, and three coincidences are a proof."

"She said that, did she," Dick replied with surprise.

"Yes, Dick. That's why you really shouldn't be so dismissive of her."

"Okay," Dick replied, holding up his hands in surrender. "That means we need to keep an open mind. It could be that all of them are connected, which would mean ..."

"What?"

"That we are up against a sinister genius who is orchestrating all of this as part of some devious plan."

"You mean we may be up against a master criminal?!" Dora exclaimed.

"Don't be alarmed, dear," Dick said, patting the back of her left hand. "It's only a remote possibility."

"I'm not alarmed, dear," Dora replied. "I'm excited."

CHAPTER SEVENTEEN

"Well, Watson, we've got a partner in our investigation," Dick said the next morning after breakfast. Watson barked as Dick continued. "Yes, Watson, Dora has decided to help. Not that we need any help, do we?" Watson barked again, either in agreement or because he wanted a biscuit. "What we've done is to divvy things up. Since Dora still has to manage the inn, she'll stick close to home, while you and I will venture farther afield. The first thing I was thinking we should do is to tail a possible suspect."

Watson barked once more. "And who might that be you ask? Why the one person who has been remarkably uninvolved in any of these strange occurrences, Pete Goudy. There's something mysterious about him including why he's come back to stay here the past few years. Maybe we can find out if we follow him, which is precisely what we are going to do. And while we are tailing him, Dora will try to find out something about his background. And, because we will both need our energy, I have some breakfast treats for both of us." Dick gave a biscuit to Watson, who immediately devoured it, while he chewed thoughtfully on a biscotti.

***

"What can you tell me about Mr. Goudy?" Dora asked Martin. They were sitting in the breakfast room having their daily meeting over a cup of coffee.

"He started coming here a few years ago. Books the same dates and the same room on the ground floor. Why are you interested in Pete?"

"We want our repeat customers, like Mr. Goudy, to know that we value their loyalty and don't want to lose them. Nothing is worse than a customer who feels they're being taken for granted. In order to do that it's helpful to know more about them than just their name, address, and credit card number."

"Pete doesn't like to talk about himself, or talk at all, for that matter." Martin rubbed his chin. "He also doesn't want anyone in his room."

"Not even for Elspeth to clean?"

"Nope. He'll ask for fresh towels, but that's it. Funny thing is when he checks out the room is clean and neat as can be."

"I wonder why he always books the same room and for the same dates."

"No idea," Martin replied, "but come to think of it he hasn't booked the room for next year. Usually, he books it when he checks in because he doesn't want to take a chance on it not being available, but he didn't this time. I'll have to ask him about it. Wouldn't want to lose one of our loyal customers, like you said."

Dora went to her office next to the reception desk. It had been the pastor's study in the former church and had escaped much of the renovation when the church was converted into the inn.

There was beveled stained glass in the top half of both of the windows that gave Dora a prismatic bath as she booted up her computer. There must be something she could find online about Pete Goudy. On the inn's guest registration his home address was a Portland post office box, so she decided to do an online search for any Pete Goudy who was living in Portland. When that proved fruitless, she expanded her search to include social media. The only social media site she used was Facebook. After logging on, she did a search, but none of the Pete Goudys or P. Goudys or just plain old Goudys was a match. Well, that would be too easy, wouldn't it, she sighed. As Dick reminded her, real detective work isn't like it is in the movies, where someone taps their computer keyboard a couple of times and all of the information they're looking for, even if it's top secret, pops up on the screen.

Dora's thoughts were interrupted by Natalya's whiny voice complaining to Martin about there not being a computer she could use. "What kind of hotel is this if it doesn't have a business center with computers?"

Calmly, Martin replied, "First of all we're an inn not a hotel, and second, most people who stay here don't have their cell-phones confiscated by their mothers. You're welcome to use our copier and printer though."

"Natalya," Dora said, "you're just the person I want to see."

"Me?" Natalya replied.

"Yes, I need your expert advice on something."

Surprised, Natalya asked, "You want my advice?" as Martin mouthed the words silently with even more surprise.

Dora walked to the open doorway of her office, "If you wouldn't mind stepping into my office, I'll explain," Dora answered, giving Martin an 'it's okay' look, to which he responded with a 'you're the boss' shrug.

"Natalya, I'm trying to improve our online marketing and I'd like your advice." Dora told herself that it wasn't really lying, because she did need advice and they should expand their presence online.

Natalya answered. "What do I know about marketing a place like this? I don't have a credit card, so I couldn't book a room here, even if I wanted to."

Ignoring the 'even if I wanted to' part of Natalya's response, Dora said, "I understand that, but as a young person you probably know a lot about social media and, I have to confess, I don't know that much about it other than Facebook."

"Ugh," Natalya said, scrunching her face. "That's for old people. It's like using the mail or a telephone. Even Twitter, which is now called X, by the way, is old-fashioned. The social media you should use are Tik Tok, Snapchat, Instagram, that sort of thing."

"What if we want to reach particular people but we don't know what social media they use? It's called target marketing."

"Sure, there's a way that you can find out what apps and website people visit regulary if you know their name."

"Can you show me?"

"If you help me with my problem."

"Of course I will. I'll let you use my computer for half an hour."

"An hour," Natalya countered.

"Forty-five minutes."

"Agreed," Natalya said, brushing past Dora and sat down in front of the computer and started typing. As Dora hovered behind Natalya, a website called Peekabyte filled the screen. It asked for a name to use for the search.

"Let's see, how about Pete Goudy?" Dora spelled the name, betting that Natalya wouldn't have a clue who Pete Goudy was. She was right, because Natalya typed in the name without batting an eye. A moment later a list of Pete Goudys appeared with the social media sites and websites they visit next to each of them.

"Is there a way to narrow down the list?"

"Sure, if you know something like where this Goudy lives, that could narrow it down."

"How about Portland?"

Natalya tapped in Pete Goudy, Portland, Oregon, and a list of three names popped up. "See, it's really simple. This is as much info as I can get on this app. So, if you want more info on the person you have to go to the social media app or website they're visiting regularly."

"I see that Pete Goudy number one and number three use more than one social media app, but number two uses only one and it's a website."

"Yeah," Natalya answered as if she had bubblegum in her mouth. "Number one and three all use social media apps I'm familiar with. Number one is definitely an oldster since he only uses Facebook, but number three uses Tik Tok, Instagram and Snapchat, which people under thirty use."

"What about number two?"

"He's the only Pete who isn't on an app but he is a frequent user of a website and it's called Black Patch. I've never heard of it."

"Can you find out anything about it?" Dora pressed. "I promise that this is the last thing I'll ask you to do and then you can have the room and computer to yourself."

"That's okay. This is sort of fun." Natalya clicked on Black Patch and a black eye patch with a skull and crossbones appeared followed by the name 'Shiver Me Timbers Society' and the warning that non-members who try to enter will be forced to walk the plank. Following the warning was a large black X .

"This is right out of *Pirates of the Caribbean*. I wonder if Johnny Depp is a member?" Natalya said, then clicked on the X.

CHAPTER EIGHTEEN

When Dick took Watson for a walk in Manhattan near their apartment, instead of a boring trip to Riverside Park, broken only by stops at fire hydrants along the way, they both liked nothing better than to tail someone. With a blood-hound like Watson who could follow someone's scent, they could stay at a distance and still not lose the person. First, they would go to Zorba the Greek's coffee shop just a half block from their place, where Dick would quickly and discreetly nab a paper napkin left behind by a person who had just finished breakfast. Outside, he would hold the napkin to Watson's nose and when the person came out after paying their bill, they'd followed them.

If the person decided to take the subway or bus, they could continue to follow them, because of the service dog vest that Watson wore. If they were stopped and questioned by the transit police about Watson's status, Dick could produce a document stating that Watson was a duly registered emotional support service dog. He had gotten the registration with the help of a psychiatrist friend and sometime colleague who attested to Dick's need for an ESA dog as essential in the treatment of an anxiety disorder. What his friend left out was that the anxiety disorder was Dick feeling anxious about losing someone he was tailing. His friend also left out that he was a forensic psychiatrist who specialized in criminology and worked with Dick on some of his cases. Once, Dick and Watson had even taken a cab after the person they were following had hailed one. Unfortunately, Watson couldn't track the person's scent without sticking his head out of the window, and the cabbie refused to lower it because it was in July and he had the air conditioning on full blast.

Compared to Manhattan with its obstacle course of crowded sidewalks and streets, not to mention buses, subways, and taxis, Dick figured that tailing someone in a small town like Ilwaco would be a breeze. He knew that Goudy didn't take his car when he went out so he must be walking to wherever he was going, and it had been easy to get a napkin that Goudy had used at breakfast. They followed him across Spruce Street, Ilwaco's main drag, to the post office, then right on Lake Street past the River City Theater where a troupe of amateur thespians puts on plays and musicals, then past the museum to First Avenue. Instead of turning left toward the port, Goudy entered a store with the name Flotsam and Jetsam stenciled across its plate glass window. Not wanting Goudy to notice him, Dick loitered outside peering through the window. The store was crammed with old nets, bottles, round glass balls of some sort, and other objects that the Pacific Ocean had tossed onto the beach. "The stuff in there brings back some fond memories of the sort of junk we found when we were scavenging for evidence in the alleys of New York, doesn't it, Watson?" Watson responded with a short bark. "Yes, I know that what you find on a beach doesn't excite your olfactory nerve the way something in a dumpster does, but you have to admit there's a certain similarity between beachcombing and dumpster diving."

Dick looked back through the window and saw Goudy speaking with two women behind the counter. One woman was in her sixties and the other in her late twenties or early thirties. They looked like they could be mother and daughter. The younger woman opened a drawer and withdrew a set of car keys. "Uh, oh," Dick whispered to Watson. "I think they might be going somewhere together and it's not on foot, and we can't hail a taxi, since there aren't any in Ilwaco. If we only knew where they were going we could go back and get our car and drive there."

Just then the older woman handed the younger one a large sun hat and tube of suntan lotion. "That's pretty compelling evidence that they're headed for the beach. Unfortunately, we don't know where on the twenty-eight miles of beach they're headed."

Watson barked at something in the street and Dick turned to see the Digbys' minivan pull up and stop. Gerald Digby was at the wheel, Martha in the passenger seat and Trevor sitting behind them. Martha lowered the window and said, "Mr. Carlson, maybe you can help us. We need a good spot on the beach where we can fly the kites we bought. As you know, we were going to go kite-flying yesterday but it was delayed by that unfortunate incident with the Ouija board."

"Not only will I tell you," Dick answered enthusiastically, I'll take you there."

"You mean follow your car?"

"No, I left my car back at the inn, so I'll ride with you. Watson here has decided that what he really wants is a walk on the beach. We can do that while you fly your kites."

"Why, that's wonderful of you," Martha answered, then turned and asked Trevor to open the minivan door for Dick and Watson. As soon as the door slid open, Watson jumped in followed by Dick, who quickly closed the door just as Goudy and the younger woman exited Flotsam and Jetsam and headed for a blue pickup truck parked in front of the Digbys' minivan. Dick stalled for time by fumbling with the seat belt until the woman got behind the wheel of the pickup and Goudy climbed into the passenger seat. As the pickup truck pulled away from the curb, Dick announced he was buckled in.

Although Dick had tailed cars before, this was the first time he'd done so when the driver of the vehicle didn't know that's what they were doing. "I'll tell you how to get to this terrific spot on the beach for kite-flying as we go," Dick told Gerald.

At the light, the pickup turned left onto the Route 100 Loop Road around Cape Disappointment. Dick instructed Gerald to do the same thing, explaining, "The beach near Cape Disappointment is much better for kite-flying than farther up the peninsula because it's not as crowded so you won't get tangled up with other kites."

They continued on Loop Road past the sign announcing that they were entering Cape Disappointment State Park until the pickup turned right into a parking area with a Beard's Hollow sign. Dick told Gerald to do the same thing. "Beard's Hollow is near the great kite-flying spot I mentioned," he said. "It's just a short walk to the beach from the parking area." After they parked Dick quickly slid the door back and he and Watson got out. Goudy and the young woman had already left the pickup and were starting to walk toward the Discovery Trail at the west end of the parking lot. The trail went west for a quarter mile past the saltwater marshland of Beard's Hollow, to the beach, and then turned right and followed the coastline north up the peninsula for seven miles.

The Digbys assembled around Dick and Watson. Gerald held a canvas beach bag with several kites protruding. "It's only about a quarter mile to the beach and it's a paved walkway," Dick announced.

"Cool," Trevor said, "I'll get my skateboard."

"We told Trevor he could only use his skateboard to get to the beach," Martha explained to Dick.

By the time Trevor retrieved his skateboard from the mini-van, Goudy and the young woman were at least a hundred yards ahead and had disappeared into the shadows cast by the Douglas firs, hemlocks, and alders that formed a canopy over the Discovery Trail. Not that Dick was worried, because Watson already had his nose to the ground, or asphalt in this case, and had picked up Goudy's scent. Dick attached a leash to Watson to keep him from running in pursuit. "He loves the ocean so if I didn't keep him on a leash he'd have taken off and swum halfway to Hawaii by the time we get to the beach."

After Trevor handed the bag with the kites to Gerald, he started off on his skateboard followed by his parents, Dick, and Watson. Ten minutes later they caught up with Trevor who was standing on his skateboard, rocking it back and forth. Next to him was a sandy path bordered by wind stunted pines that Dick knew led to the beach. Watson started for the path, tugging at the leash, and Dick knew that Goudy and the woman had taken it instead of continuing on the trail. "This path goes to the beach and that great spot for kite-flying," Dick said.

"It doesn't feel very windy for kite-flying," Trevor said, then added hopefully, "Maybe I can just skateboard on this paved trail instead."

"That's because the trees are blocking the wind," Dick replied. "Once we get out in the open on the beach there will be plenty of wind."

"Besides, Trevor, we said we were going to fly kites as a family," Martha said.

"If you all had skateboards we could do that as a family instead," Trevor mumbled as he picked up his board and followed them onto the sandy path.

After a couple of minutes they emerged from the trees and stood on a grass-covered dune looking out upon a vista of sand, surf, ocean, and puffy clouds drifting across a deep blue sky. The wind carried the roar of the pounding waves as it bent the seagrass. On the beach, a handful of adults and kids were flying kites that swooped up and down. Several other kids and adults were running in and out of the surf, while small children were building subdivisions in the sand, watched over by parents in beach chairs. Goudy and the woman walked toward a massive jumble of rocks at the base of the Cape Disappointment headland known as the Fishing Rocks. Dick couldn't see anyone fishing off the rocks, but there were a couple of anglers in waders casting into the waves.

As Gerald and Trevor started to put one of the kites together, Dick told them that he and Watson were going to walk along the beach to the Fishing Rocks.

Dick and Watson stayed far enough behind Goudy and the woman that Goudy wouldn't have been able to make out who they were even if he had turned around. Goudy and his companion continued until they reached the rocks at the base of the headland cliff. Since the tide was out, they were able to step directly from the beach onto the rocks. Slowly the two made their way across the rugged, foam-slick rocks, sending scores of seagulls into the air, and continued toward the leading edge of the headland that sent up a spray of water like the bow of some fossilized ship.

"Obviously, they can only reach wherever it is they're going on those rocks when the tide is out," Dick said to Watson who barked in agreement. About twenty minutes later Goudy and the woman reappeared and retraced their route across the rocks back to the beach.

Dick said to Watson, "We'll have to come back another time to find out where they went. Right now, we need to get back to the Digbys before we're spotted. The problem is, Goudy still might notice us since the Digbys are flying their kites near the trailhead."

When they got closer to the Digbys, Dick saw that they had managed to get three kites aloft. However, Gerald was controlling two kites and Martha one and Trevor was nowhere to be seen.

Seeing Dick, Martha laughed and said, "Now that I know how much fun it is, I won't be offended the next time someone tells me to go fly a kite."

"Where's Trevor?" Dick asked.

"He got bored, so we told him he could go back to the trail and skateboard, then meet us in an hour at the parking lot."

"Do you mind if I use his kite? I haven't flown one in years."

"Sure, here," Gerald answered and handed Dick the line for a diamond shaped multicolored kite with a long tail streaming behind it.

Dick took the end of the line and flew the kite for a minute until he noticed that Goudy and the woman were approaching and would soon be close enough to recognize him and Watson. Finding the Digbys flying kites was one thing, but seeing Dick and Watson there as well might be enough to arouse Goudy's suspicion. Dick quickly jerked the line so that the kite started flying erratically, stalled and went into a dive, spiraling into the sand fifty yards up the beach. "Darn," Dick shouted to Martha and Gerald, then ran toward the kite that was thrashing about in the wind.

Watson outran Dick and leapt up in the air and grabbed one of the kite tails in his teeth then wrestled the kite to the sand where he held it down with one paw as it flopped around as if trying to escape. "Great work, Watson," Dick said, then knelt and seemed to check the kite for damage while he followed Goudy and the woman's progress out of the corner of his eye. When Goudy and the woman reached the trail and were walking away from the beach, Dick told Watson to let go of the tail that was still in the firm grip of his clenched teeth. "We've finished our tailing for the day, Watson."

CHAPTER NINETEEN

"You look like you've gotten some sun," Dora said to Dick after he and Watson returned to the inn.

"We were at the beach flying kites."

Dora crossed her arms. "Flying kites at the beach, and here I thought you were following our Mr. Goudy."

"I was," Dick replied. "Watson and I tailed him to a shop downtown called Flotsam and Jetsam."

"I've been meaning to pay them a visit to see if they have anything that might add to our nautical decor."

"I imagine there might be, but I didn't go inside. I just observed Goudy through the window as he spoke with the two women who work there, and then he left with the younger of the two."

"That would be Bridgette and the older woman would be her mother, Muriel. I met them at their booth at the open-air market the port has on Saturday morning."

"What was your impression?" Dick asked.

"Bridgette seemed a bit adrift, but I suppose that means she's well-suited for being the one who combs the beaches for the flotsam and jetsam that they sell. What happened when they left the shop?"

"They got into a pickup truck and headed off with Bridgette driving."

"But how did you follow them since you didn't have a car?"

Dick filled Dora in on hitching a ride with the Digbys to Beard's Hollow and then, after leaving the Digbys to fly their kites, how he and Watson followed Goudy and Bridgette to the Fishing Rocks. "One minute I could see them on the rocks and then they just disappeared. They reappeared about twenty minutes later."

"Where do you think they disappeared to?"

"I'll just have to go back to the Fishing Rocks and see what I can find out."

Dora quickly admonished Dick, "It's not a good idea to go climbing around the Fishing Rocks by yourself. They're slippery and those sneaker waves can carry you away."

"Watson will be with me." Watson, who had been napping at their feet, lifted his head and barked. "See, he's raring to go."

Dora looked at Watson, "With all due respect to your abilities, Watson, swimming isn't one of them, is it?" Watson let out a whimper and buried his saggy face in his paws. Dora turned to Dick, "See, Watson agrees with me."

"Then he can wait on the beach and get help if anything happens to me."

"By the time Watson finds someone and is somehow able to communicate to them that you're in trouble, the riptide will have taken you out to sea and the current would then carry you all the way to the Aleutian Islands."

Dick grinned, "Maybe I'd be lucky and end up on a beach in Hawaii, instead."

"Really, Dick, it's not funny."

"I'll take my cellphone so I can call the Coast Guard and they can send a helicopter."

"A lot of good your cellphone will do if it's soaked in salt water, and who knows if there's even service at the Fishing Rocks."

"All right, all right," Dick said holding both hands up in surrender. "Then who do you suggest should accompany me?"

"I think that Lars would be the perfect person. He grew up here and he told me that he's worked on a fishing boat, so he should know his way around the ocean."

"He is our handyman so he might come in handy," Dick admitted, then asked, "And what have you been up to?"

"Well, honey, while you and Watson were tailing Goudy on the beach, I was surfing the internet with Natalya ..."

"Natalya?"

"Yes, Natalya, she offered to help me in exchange for me letting her use my computer. Her mom confiscated her cellphone. Under the circumstances I thought it was worth the trade-off. I said I wanted to know about how we could improve our online marketing of the inn and I gave her Goudy's name as the type of person we would want to market to, figuring that she wouldn't know he was one of the guests."

"Since all of us old fogeys are the same."

"Something like that, except only another old fogey would know what that word means. Anyway, she used this online tool I'd never heard of called Peekabyte that's spelled b-y-t-e, which is sort of cute. It can find what apps and websites people use on the internet."

"And what did you find?"

"He doesn't use social media sites, but it so happens Goudy is interested in pirates and buried treasure because we found him on the website for the Shiver Me Timbers Society, which has a skull and crossbones on its home page and an X."

"A Jolly Roger seems a fitting greeting for a pirate portal," Dick said. "Were you able to find out anything about this society?"

"Other than the name and the skull and crossbones there was nothing on the home page. We couldn't get any farther without being a member with a password. It was really ingenious because it showed a person being forced to walk a plank and being prodded by the blade of a cutlass. If the password was wrong the cutlass poked the person's back and they went into the water where there were swarms of shark circling about. We tried a couple of passwords that we thought someone interested in pirates might use, but they weren't correct, and the person ended up being pushed off the end of the plank followed by the water turning blood red." Dora stopped and shivered.

"Died of shark bytes, huh?" Dick said. "That's spelled 'b-y-t-e'."

"I get the joke," Dora said. "But it was gruesome just the same."

"So, you weren't able to find out anything more about this society and Goudy's involvement?"

"Not yet," Dora replied. "But Natalya used my computer to send the website's address to some of her friends and they are going to try and find a password that will allow us to get into the site. She's really quite excited about it."

"Martin told me that Goudy knows a lot about pirates," Dick said.

"Maybe he comes back here every year so he can indulge his hobby? "

Dick nodded, "Yes, dear, assuming that there were pirates plying the waters around here." Dick poked Watson gently with the toe of his shoe. "Well, Watson, before we go for another walk on the beach we need to see our floating historian about pirates."

Dick and Watson proceeded to walk down to the Port where they found Morgan Murray sitting in a canvas deck chair on his boat drinking a bottle of Cape D Dark Ale. Morgan told him to take a seat wherever he could find a spot. To Dick's question about pirates operating in the area, Morgan answered with an emphatic yes, followed by, "And I don't mean the *Goonies*."

"Who were the goonies?" Dick asked.

"The *Goonies* is a movie filmed in Astoria in 1985 about some kids who discover the stolen treasure of One-Eyed Willy, a pirate who hid his treasure in a sea cave. Not in a chest, mind you, but in his pirate ship named *The Inferno*. In addition to One-Eyed Willy's booby traps they also had to fight off a gang of modern-day villains. People from all over the world still come to Astoria to visit locations where the movie was shot, especially the 'Goonie House' where two of the kids who were brothers lived." Morgan paused for a loud belch. "I'm surprised you don't know all about it since it's such a tourist attraction."

"Sounds like it's for kids."

"Kids," Morgan laughed heartily. "It's the adults who saw the movie when they were kids who are the big fans. Customers on my fishing charters are always asking me to point out the pirate cave where the Goonies found *The Inferno* with its treasure."

"What do you tell them?"

"Why I tell them I'd be happy to if they charter my boat to take them all the way down the coast to Hollywood, California."

"You said that you didn't mean the *Goonies* when you said there were pirates around here: Then who did you mean?"

"The most famous was Sir Francis Drake."

"Drake was a pirate?"

"Indeed he was, although he came to the Pacific Northwest on a secret commission by Queen Elizabeth I to find the waterway that was believed to connect the Atlantic to the Pacific. He never found it of course, since there never was one until the

Panama Canal was dug four hundred years later and 3,600 miles south of here. However, El Draque – the dragon as he was called by the Spanish whose ships he plundered from California to Vancouver Island near Seattle – accumulated quite a fortune."

"Did he bury any of it?"

"As far as we know, he took it all back to England. He had to give the Queen her share, after all." Morgan stopped and took another swig of ale. "Although you never know. It wouldn't be the first time someone hid money that was due the government."

"I imagine that in Elizabethan England the penalty for treasure tax evasion would have been off with the head not a slap on the wrist."

Morgan gave a wicked smile, "In hindsight, or in this case *Golden Hind* sight, since that was the name of his ship, when Drake was dying of dysentery he might well have welcomed an executioner's axe to put him out of his misery."

"What about pirates who, unlike Drake, were just infamous?"

"If you mean someone who was more in the blackhearted scoundrel mold of the pirates of the Caribbean, such as Blackbeard, there was Iron Jim Sallow. He preyed on ships along the Washington Coast. Supposedly, he buried his stolen treasure in the vicinity of present day Seattle. Unfortunately for Sallow, the map he made showing where it was buried was stolen by a member of his crew and he disappeared while chasing the thief. Neither was heard from again. As far as we know the treasure is still buried unless some construction workers found it while excavating for one of those Seattle skyscrapers and never reported it." Morgan chuckled, "I think the Space Needle would be a perfect 'x marks the spot'."

Do you think he could have buried it around here instead of Seattle?"

"It's possible, but his home waters were up in the San Juan Islands near Seattle, so it's unlikely."

"What about pirates who operated in the waters around Cape Disappointment?"

Morgan shrugged, "When it comes to the pirates who operated in the waters around here, it seems that infamy is as fleeting as fame, because most of their names and exploits remain as buried as their treasures. Unfortunately for us historians, the pirate saying that 'dead men tell no tales' turns out to be true."

Dick could hardly hide his disappointment as he pondered his half-empty bottle of ale, but perked up when Morgan said, "Now, one could say that Captain Johnson was a pirate if the stories about his treasure and how he got it are true."

"You didn't call him a pirate when I was here before."

"Ah, but you wanted to know about the unsolved murders I wrote about in my book, not pirates. However, the definition of a pirate is someone who commits a robbery and engages in violence on the sea or the shores of the sea, so if Johnson did what he was suspected of, in addition to being a thief and murderer, you could add pirate to his unsavory pedigree. You know, after this conversation, I've got half a mind to make pirates and buried treasure the subject of my next book." Morgan downed the rest of his ale. "In fact, I think I'll open another bottle to celebrate that idea."

CHAPTER TWENTY

Dora was sitting with Nicole at one of the dining room tables, reviewing how things had gone for the first breakfast served at the inn by Cape D'Lite, the name of Nicole's new catering business.

"What did you think?" Nicole asked, unable to hide her anxiety.

"I thought it went very, very well." Dora would have gushed if she was a gusher, so two 'verys' would have to convey how pleased she was. "I loved the omelet I had, and Dick devoured the pancakes. And the coffee was so good that I actually had two cups. The guests all seemed very pleased as well. What I don't understand is how you were able to do all of it by yourself?"

"Oh, but I'm not working by myself. My boyfriend, Zeke, is helping. He's my partner in Cape D'Lite. We thought we'd have to figure out some way to persuade his parents to back us, but now, because of this arrangement, we don't need them."

Dora gave Nicole a pat on her right hand. "I'm glad we saved you from that. It wouldn't be right to have them risk their retirement savings."

Nicole laughed and rolled her eyes, "Zeke's parents are loaded. Money isn't a problem, I am."

"You?"

"They think I've ruined his future. Lured him away from his true destiny. The only way they would have agreed to give us any money is for us to be just business partners rather than, well you know. They thought he was having a fling and certainly never imagined that we would still be together."

"I take it you've been together a long time?"

"We met seven years ago, in the summer between our junior and senior years in high school."

Dora clapped her hands, "You were high school sweethearts!"

"We didn't go to the same high school. Zeke is from San Francisco and went to a private school there, and I went to the high school over in Astoria. That's where my family is from. As I said, Zeke's family is loaded. His father is a venture capitalist who funds Silicon Valley start-ups."

"Your catering business is a start-up."

"Oh, we're low-tech. Now if we had robots cooking, instead of a human being like me, it would be different. To get back to how we met, Zeke's family would sail up here every summer in their humongous yacht. His father fancies himself as a sailor, but Zeke says he just sits on the bridge drinking beers while the captain and crew do all the work. I was working that summer as a waitress at the Scuttlebutt Cafe, which was where the Grist and Grind is now, and that's how we met. The plan for Zeke was to go to Stanford, get a degree in business, and then go to work for his father."

"And meeting you derailed all of that?"

"Instead of Stanford he went to Oregon State, which is also where I was studying culinary arts, and instead of a degree in business, he got a degree in philosophy, and instead of moving back to the Bay Area, he moved in with me in an old RV we bought, and instead of going into his father's business funding start-ups, he's started his own business with me."

"I imagine that his father will be proud of Zeke now that he isn't asking him for money."

"Hardly. It just reminds his father that he depends on his family fortune to bankroll his venture capital business. You see, Zeke's great-grandfather owned a bunch of warehouses on the San Francisco waterfront that turned out later to be sitting on some of the most valuable land in San Francisco. His grand-father developed the property into prime real estate and then sold the property at the height of the real estate boom for a gazillion dollars. That's the source of the money that he invests in start-ups, not what he made on his own. As Zeke says, for all his talk about venture capitalism and taking risks, his dad made his money the old-fashioned way, by inheriting it. What Zeke is doing reminds his dad of what he didn't do." Nicole shrugged and arched her eyebrows. "Anyway, Zeke just told his parents that he doesn't want any money from them. Now he's as penniless as me, which gives us an additional incentive to make Cape D'Lite a success. We can't tell you how grateful we are that you are helping us by letting us use the kitchen and also allowing us to park our RV behind the inn so we don't have to keep paying through the nose to rent a spot in a trailer park."

Dora couldn't help but feel akin to Nicole since they were both starting a new business. Two women entrepreneurs. Despite their ages and life backgrounds, she felt that she and Nicole weren't all that different. On the other hand, Dora couldn't see any similarities between Dick and Zeke. She wondered what it would be like to swap business partners? With a smile on her face, she said, "I'm happy that you're happy, and that things have been going smoothly. We want to make this a success as much as you do, so if you have any problems, let me know right away."

"There is one thing that happened last night I should mention," Nicole said. "We worked until after midnight rearranging everything in the kitchen to make it more efficient and setting up for breakfast and..." Nicole paused and bit her lip.

"And?"

"And we heard some strange noises."

"Like what?"

"It sounded like scraping and digging."

Alarmed, Dora asked, "Someone was digging outside?"

"Not from outside, but under the kitchen and the dining room where we are now. We're concerned that there might be mice or even rats in the basement. We would have checked it out but we couldn't find the basement door."

'There isn't a door."

"Then how do you access it?"

"There's nothing to access because there's no basement under here."

"Are you sure, because the noises were definitely coming from under us."

"It is an old building, with lots of squeaks and creaks."

"It wasn't that kind of noise. Maybe there's a crawl space under here. Mice or even rats don't need much room. If they get inside, the health department will shut us down. The port has a bit of a rat problem, and that's why the Grist and Grind has an exterminator come monthly. Maybe some of the rats made their way up here."

***

"First we have bats in the belfry, and now we have rats in the basement," Dick said, after Dora told him about her conversation with Nicole.

"But there is no basement," Dora answered. "And we don't know for certain if the sounds that they heard came from rats. It could be mice or raccoons or squirrels or, I can't believe I'm saying this, a ghost."

"But why would a ghost be under the floor of the kitchen and dining room?" Dick asked.

"I don't know, maybe there's a ghost basement. You know, like those 'man caves' with a bar and big screen TV you men have in basements where you hang out with your friends."

"I never had one," Dick retorted.

"That's only because the basement in our building in New York was twelve floors below our apartment and the only man hanging out in it was Fred, the building superintendent."

"Then maybe I should find this mystery basement so I can hang out there with or without ghosts."

Dora rolled her eyes. "Very funny, dear."

"I'm serious, honey. Watson and I can venture down into the depths beneath the inn and discover who or what is hanging out there. What do you say to a little subterranean sleuthing, Watson?" Watson barked and wagged his tail.

"First we need to find out if we really have anything under the inn to venture down to," Dora said. "There's certainly nothing that shows up in the plans for the inn and just to make sure I called Farley and he said he didn't find any sign of something under the dining area when he was renovating the place into an inn. Still, Nicole and her boyfriend Zeke are certain that the noise came from under the kitchen and dining room, so we have to do something."

"We could rip up the floor. I bet Lars is pretty good with a crowbar."

"There must be a less destructive way, Dick. The dining room has the original oak floor and we can't go tearing up the tile in the kitchen."

"How about Thistlewaite and his gang of ghostbusters?" Dick asked.

"They might be able to find out if something supernatural is making the noise, but I don't know if they would be able to tell us if there is a basement or crawl space. Still, it doesn't hurt to ask."

***

"As a matter of fact," Cedric said, after Dora and Dick presented him with their problem as they sat at one of the tables in the dining room, "the old houses and buildings we investigate are filled with secret spaces where the paranormal might be lurking. Our GPR can tell us if there's a basement or crawl space beneath here."

"What does GPR stand for?" Dora asked, pouring some tea from the fresh pot she'd made into Cedric's cup.

After taking a sip of tea and nodding that it met his taste test, Cedric replied. "It stands for ground penetrating radar. GPR is used in a number of ways from locating underground utility lines to examining archeological ruins to finding what's hidden behind the walls of old houses and buildings."

"Can GPR detect ghosts as well?" Dora asked.

"Of course not," Cedric shook his head. "Radar waves would go right through them. That's why they're apparitions. We will deploy our GPR to see if there is a hidden space under your dining room and kitchen. At the same time, we will employ our sound detection equipment to see if we can detect the source of the noises that scared your cook."

"Chef," Dora corrected him.

"Is there a difference?"

"I'm surprised that you didn't taste the difference at breakfast this morning. It was our chef's debut."

"I skipped it. The paranormal occurrences we investigate usually take place late at night, so it wasn't until dawn that we finished our work. I was sound asleep during your breakfast. In fact, if we want to hear the noises your..." Cedric paused, and then said, "your chef and her assistant..."

"Zeke is her partner," Dora said.

"Okay, your chef and her partner ... Zeke ..."

"He's her business partner as well as her boyfriend, and our chef's name is Nicole."

"Does it really make a difference that I know their name and business and personal relationship?" Cedric snapped.

"No need to get testy, Thistlewaite," Dick said, feeling the need to provide some spousal support.

"Sorry, must be from lack of sleep," Cedric answered. "Anyway, if Nicole, your chef, and Zeke, her business and domestic partner, heard these noises late last night, then we'll need to start at the same time."

"They heard the sound of scraping and digging so if that's what you hear tonight, it won't tell you whether a ghost is doing it or some other critter," Dora pointed out.

"But remember, dear," Dick said. "Cedric and his colleagues use some sort of high tech equipment that picks up sounds beyond the range of the human ear, right Cedric?"

"Your husband is correct," Cedric said, emphasizing husband. "We use an electronic voice phenomena system that enables us to pick up sounds that are outside the range of the human ear."

"But what if the only sound is digging and scraping?" Dora said, undeterred by Cedric and Dick's mansplaining. "Does it tell you if a ghost is using some tool or their fingernails, which are probably as long as knife blades?"

"I'm afraid the sounds made by paranormal phenomena engaging in digging or scraping aren't in our database."

"Then this might be your chance to remedy that deficiency," Dora replied, triumphantly.

"Yes, I suppose it might be," Cedric admitted, grudgingly. "Although that will depend on what we find when we enter the space. That is if our GPR detects that there is indeed a hidden space beneath your kitchen and dining room from where such sounds are emanating."

"Why do you have to get inside the space?" Dick asked.

"Because regardless of whether or not we can determine what is causing the sounds, we will need to enter it in order to do a thorough investigation." Cedric finished his tea. "I must admit that we paranormal investigators live for the opportunity to enter a secret room or passageway. It's similar to the feeling that the famous archeologist Howard Carter must have felt when he discovered King Tut's tomb."

"I just hope you aren't disappointed if you discover mice instead of mummies," Dick cracked, with an echoing bark from Watson.

"But if there is a space how do we enter it?" Dora asked. "We can't find any entrance."

"If it were easy to discover, it wouldn't be a hidden space, would it? That's part of the challenge and the fun," Cedric said, rubbing his hands together with relish.

CHAPTER TWENTY ONE

With Dick and Lars, along with Watson, having left on their expedition to the Fishing Rocks, Dora turned her attention to future bookings. Dora stood behind Martin who sat at the front desk computer. As he scrolled through their reservations it was clear that reservations looked fairly strong until Labor Day. "Summer is the busiest time of year here. That's the time when people plan ahead to come here for a vacation," Martin commented. He scrolled down and when he reached September the number of reservations began to drop. "As you can see, after Labor Day advance bookings begin to decline, especially midweek. There are fewer planned vacations and the ones people do plan tend to be either to somewhere warm like Florida or cold like a ski resort."

"If only people could add wet and windy to hot and cold places for their winter vacation," Dora said, half-joking.

Martin nodded. "The trips people do take here are on the weekends and tend to be last-minute decisions based on the weather, which tends to get increasingly unpredictable until Thanksgiving, after which it becomes completely unpredictable. That's why everyone lowers their room rates after Labor Day, and even more so during the winter. Some of the hotels close completely until April."

"Yes, I did my due diligence and know that the room rates will be lower. What bothers me is not knowing what our occupancy rate will be."

Martin shrugged, "That's just the way it is, I'm afraid."

"Then we need to do something about it," Dora declared with a firmness that surprised her as much as Martin.

"Like what?"

"Like events that would attract advance bookings. We have the old sanctuary that we could use, and Nicole can cater. Now we need some ideas." Dora looked at Martin, expectantly.

"Weddings?" Martin ventured. "We've had a few of them, but we never promoted the inn as a place for weddings."

"Great idea, Martin," Dora answered. "Destination weddings are quite popular. The problem is most weddings are held during the summer and that's not when we need guests. Same goes for family reunions and things like that." She didn't mention the idea of destination funerals since she'd decided to bury the idea after her conversation with Dick. "What about festivals?"

"Most of them are in the summer as well," Martin replied. "The only big event in the winter I can think of is the Fisher Poet Festival in Astoria in February."

"What's that?"

"It's when people gather to hear poems about fishing."

"There are poems about fishing?"

Martin nodded his head, "Sort of like that book about a white whale..."

"You mean Moby Dick."

"That's the one. It's pretty famous. We have a copy in the parlor and I've been meaning to read it when I have the time."

"You'll need lots of time," Dora laughed. "Dick's the only person I know who read all of Moby Dick. I see your point that if Melville can write a great book about trying to catch a white whale, then people can write poems about fishing for salmon. If nothing else, they're bound to be shorter and funnier than Moby Dick. However, since a poetry festival about fishing is already taken by our friends across the river, we need to think of some other festival or event that might attract people to our side."

"Why not pirates and buried treasure?" A girl's voice asked.

"Who's that?" Martin jumped in his chair, startled by the unexpected voice coming from Dora's office. They both looked through the doorway at the multicolored hair visible above the computer screen.

"I forgot that Natalya is using my computer," Dora explained, then entered the office.

"My friends were able to hack the Shiver Me Timbers website," Natalya announced turning the computer screen so that Dora could see.

"What's Shiver Me Timbers?" Martin asked. He had followed Dora and was looking over her shoulder at the screen.

Thinking it would be better to make up a cover story than to let Martin know about her and Dick's suspicions regarding Goudy, Dora replied, "Natalya was showing me how we could improve our marketing by using online tools and I asked her to demonstrate by finding more background on one of our regular guests, Mr. Goudy. She was able to find out that he's a member of something called the Shiver Me Timbers Society. Perhaps by learning more about this group we can target our marketing to reach more people like Goudy."

"Me and some friends were able to find a way to get into their website without having a password," Natalya said with more than a little pride at her accomplishment.

"Isn't that illegal?" Martin asked.

Natalya gave Martin a 'you're so square' look. "We're not stealing anything."

"But if they catch you..."

"I guess they'll make us walk the plank," she deadpanned, then erupted in laughter. "A cyber plank. Don't worry. I'll let them know that we were just testing their security and that it sucks. Anonymously, of course. They should thank us for doing them a favor."

"Now that we're inside their site, what can we find out about Goudy?" Dora asked.

Natalya scrolled through a menu and clicked on 'Pirate Profiles.'

"They all have weird pirate names," Natalya said.

"Do any of them have Pete in the name?" Dora asked.

"There's a Peg Leg Pete." Natalya clicked on the name and a photo of Pete Goudy appeared with a red pirate scarf covering his head and a large golden ring hanging from his right ear.

"He's no Johnny Depp, but he looks cooler here than he does in person," Natalya said.

"Can you print his profile?" Dora asked.

"Aye, aye," Natalya replied and hit the print button.

"I wonder if there are any members of this group who live around here?"

"It doesn't look like they list them by where they live," Natalya replied.

"Can you type in the name Bridgette and see if anything comes up?"

"Who's Bridgette?" Natalya asked.

"The daughter of Muriel Binsberry who owns a local shop."

"You know Bridgette and Muriel?" Martin asked.

"All I know is that Bridgette's mother, Muriel, owns Flotsam and Jetsam. Is there anything more you can tell me about her and her daughter?"

Martin scratched his right cheek and answered, "Muriel and her late husband Ellsworth were both high school teachers in

Portland and came here for a month every summer for years. They spent most of their time beachcombing. When Ellsworth retired a few years ago they moved here and bought the old Helsinki Hall."

"Helsinki as in Helsinki, Finland?" Dora asked.

Martin nodded and said, "A lot of Scandinavians immigrated here. They worked in the canneries and fishing, and they all had their social clubs, and this one was, as the name implies, for those of Finnish descent. The membership shrank over the years and the building got to be too much for the members to maintain, so they closed it. Turns out there's not much demand for a building like that, so it was vacant for a dozen years until the Binsberrys purchased it. I'll tell you, people were really relieved since it was beginning to be an eyesore. Although it was a bit of a surprise that they bought Helsinki Hall, it was no surprise when they opened Flotsam and Jetsam given their love of beachcombing. A year after it opened Ellsworth died in a tragic accident when he fell in the ocean."

"Was he eaten by a great white shark?" Natalya asked, hopefully.

"No, he was on the Fishing Rocks and apparently slipped and was carried out to sea by the riptide. They found his body a couple of days later washed up in Dead Man's Cove."

"Like a piece of flotsam," Dora said.

"More than one person said those very words at the time. Mind you, it wasn't disrespectful since Ellsworth was so fond of flotsam. Muriel put his ashes in a watertight container and paid a crew member of a freighter going to Japan to toss it off the ship in the middle of the Pacific." Martin chuckled. "Who knows what beach he'll end up on."

"What about the Bridgette?"

"Bridgette came here to live with Muriel after Ellsworth died. She helps out with the store as well. I don't know what she did before that. She and Muriel just said that she was off seeing the world."

Natalya quickly typed in Bridgette. A page with the heading Buccaneer Bridgette popped up with a photo of a young woman dressed in pirate garb with brightly rouged cheeks, thick black mascara and a magenta pirate scarf on her head that looked to be much more expensive than the one Goudy was wearing in his photo.

"That's Bridgette," Martin said. "How did you know that she and Pete were both members of this pirate group?"

"Dick said that Goudy stopped at Flotsam and Jetsam and that a young woman drove him to Beard's Hollow," Dora replied.

"How did he know that?"

Although she felt guilty, Dora continued with her cover up. "Dick and Watson went on a walk around town this morning and they saw Mr. Gaudy enter the shop and then they came out and, as I said, Bridgette drove them both to Beard's Hollow. Dick decided to investigate what they were up to – being a criminologist he can't help himself, so he and Watson decided to follow them. They were able to get a ride with the Digbys who just happened to be passing by and were going to the beach to fly kites. At Beard's Hollow, Goudy and Bridgette parked and walked to the Fishing Rocks. Goudy and Bridgette disappeared behind the headland for about twenty minutes. Dick is going back out there to try and find out what they were doing while they were out of his sight."

"I hope he's careful because those rocks can be treacherous," Martin said. "Look what happened to old Ellsworth and he knew his way around those rocks. I always warn our guests about climbing on them because you can slip into the water just like he did or be swept off by the waves."

"That's why I made him take Lars with him."

"So that's where Lars snuck off to. I've been trying to find him. There's a leaky faucet in Room Four that needs to be..."

"I bet there's buried treasure hidden in those rocks," Natalya blurted, interrupting Martin. She had been listening impatiently while Dora and Martin talked.

"If there were, I think some fisherman would have found it long ago," Martin answered, curtly.

"Then why would two members of the Shiver Me Timbers Society be sneaking around some rocks covered in bird poop?"

CHAPTER TWENTY TWO

It was a beautiful day for a seaside stroll Dick thought, and since it was low tide, there was plenty of beach and they wouldn't have to wade through the surf to climb onto the Fishing Rocks. They weren't the only ones. There were people surf fishing, families flying kites, kids building sandcastles, and dogs scampering around on the sand. "Looks like a busy day at the beach," he said to Lars. "Smart idea to suggest we disguise ourselves as fishermen." They were both carrying fishing rods that Lars had pulled from the bed of his pickup truck. Lars had also donned a large fisherman's vest with hooks, lines, sinkers, and lures stuffed into its numerous pockets. "Otherwise, we'd stick out like sore thumbs."

"Besides, we might even catch something," Lars replied then pointed at a bald eagle circling overhead. "He sure hopes we do because he's planning to snatch it right off the hook. Good thing we aren't carrying live bait or he'd go for that as well."

"Eagles do that?" Dick said with alarm.

Lars laughed, "It's the eagle's version of catch and release. You catch the fish and he releases it ... right into his mouth. That's why you have to get your fish into a net fast." He patted the net that dangled from the vest. "And not let it flop around on the beach, or rocks in this case."

"Watson might have other ideas," Dick said nodding to Watson who was tracking the eagle with his eyes.

"I wouldn't advise him to take on an eagle in a fish fight. Once they get their talons into a fish, he'd drag Watson right into the ocean rather than let go and there aren't any doggy lifeguards around."

"I haven't seen any lifeguards, period," said Dick.

"The only lifeguard around here would be a rescue swimmer who has jumped out of a U.S. Coast Guard helicopter," Lars said holding up his cellphone, which was in a waterproof pouch hanging from his neck. Dick had left his in the truck so it wouldn't get wet. "I've got their number on speed dial, but I wouldn't bet on the Coast Guard coming out to rescue a dog."

Dick stooped down to pet Watson, "Hear that, Watson. No fetching or fighting."

Watson barked but kept his eyes on the eagle. "On second thought, I think it would be better if Watson stayed on the beach." He tugged the reluctant bloodhound over to a large log that had been swept onto the beach from a storm and secured the end of the leash to it. "You stand guard, Watson, and if we don't come back bark for help." Watson barked twice in response and sat down on the sand.

Dick returned to Lars who was at the base of the Fishing Rocks assembling the two fishing rods. "I'm not much of a fisherman," Dick said. "So show me how to cast so I don't look like a complete ass."

After some rudimentary instruction and several practice casts on the beach, Lars judged that Dick was now only a half-ass rather than a complete one. They clambered onto the Fishing Rocks. Traversing the rocks, they somehow managed to avoid the spray from the crashing waves and the bird droppings from the seagulls. The fishermen on the rocks glanced at them as they passed, but quickly returned their attention to hooking the big one. As they got closer to what had appeared at a distance to be a sheer wall of rock rising a couple of hundred feet, Lars shouted from in front, his voice barely audible above the roar of the waves, that there was a narrow path at its base. When Dick caught up to Lars, he said, "Bridgette and Goudy must have taken this path."

"Where do you think it goes?" Lars asked.

"That's what we're here to find out," Dick replied handing Lars his fishing rod. "Look, you stay here and pretend that you're fishing while I follow the path." A wave suddenly hit the rocks sending a fountain of spray.

"You're sure you want to do this?" Lars asked, wiping the water from his face.

"It can't be worse than walking on a crowded sidewalk in Manhattan and getting hit by water from an open fire hydrant."

"I think being washed into the ocean is a lot worse than a gutter."

"You haven't seen a New York gutter," Dick replied just as another wave crashed against the rocks dousing both of them.

Lars dropped the rods on the rocks and grabbed Dick before he slipped off the foam covered rocks. "I think I should go with you," he said. "That way if you get washed into the ocean I can call the Coast Guard with my cellphone." He fingered the strap around his neck that was attached to the waterproof bag.

"What happens if you end up in the ocean instead of me? Remember, I left my cellphone in your truck so I can't call for help."

"Like I told you I have the Coast Guard on speed dial. Even if I'm in the water all I have to do is punch the # key and I can do that without taking the phone out of the bag. I tested it out in my shower."

"There's a big difference between a shower and calling while trying to keep your head above the water," Dick pointed out.

"That's why this is also a life preserver," Lars smiled broadly as he tugged at the fishing vest he was wearing. "And if I pull this tab here," he put his right hand on a cord with a ring at the end, "there's a beacon with a strobe light that pops out of this pocket here," He pointed at one of the many pockets. "I'd be crazy to be climbing on these rocks without this on."

Now he tells me, Dick thought. "Fortunately, I'm a strong swimmer," he boasted, leaving out that his swimming was doing laps in the pool of the fitness club they'd belonged to in Manhattan, and the only waves were from other swimmers. "Just the same why don't you lead the way."

Slowly Dick followed Lars as they crept along the narrow path cut into the weathered sea cliff of the headland, the waves nipping at their legs. Fortunately, they were aided by the wind from the ocean that pushed them against the rough basalt surface rather than out to sea. When they reached the leading edge of the headland that projected out like the bow of a ship, the path narrowed. Lars disappeared around the corner and Dick stopped, debating whether he should continue or retreat, when Lar's right arm appeared from behind the rock wall and the index finger of his hand curled, signaling for Dick to follow. Dick edged forward, his back to the ocean and his eyes fixed on the face of the cliff until he rounded the corner. Turning his head, he looked down on a sheltered cove carved out of the rocky headland where Lars stood on a small sandy beach, a grin on his face. Dick made his way down from the path and across the mix of sand and driftwood to where Lars stood.

"The tide is going to start coming in soon and this will all be underwater, us included," Lars said after Dick had joined him.

"Then we need to start looking."

"What exactly are we looking for?"

"A hiding place. My working hypothesis is that they came here to find a pirate's buried treasure."

"You're sure giving your hypothesis a workout," Lars shook his head. "Don't pirates mark the spot where they bury their treasure with an X?"

"On pirate maps, but we don't have a map. The good news is that it's probably hidden in a place that doesn't require any climbing. I imagine they'd also pick a spot that would only be accessible at low tide, not to mention that the incoming tides would wash away any footprints in the sand. How high do you think the water gets when there's a high tide?"

"There's more than one high tide every day, but I'd say they average about six feet."

"I'm five eleven," Dick said. "So we should look for an opening in the rock that's below the top of my head. "You look on that side of the cove and I'll search on this side and hopefully we can find it before the tide starts coming in."

Dick and Lars began searching the rock wall that surrounded the cove on three sides. Fifteen minutes later they met in the back of the cove. "I found some spots where you might be able to hide an egg, but that's all," Lars announced, sitting down on a large boulder at the rear of the cove and resting his back against the cliff wall.

"Since they were hunting treasure not Easter eggs," Dick said, looking around with his hands on his hips. "Where would someone hide a treasure?"

"Search me," Lars replied from his perch.

"You seem to have found the only place in the cove to sit."

"The seat is hard on the butt and round not flat," Lars replied rapping on the boulder with the knuckles of his right hand. "But luckily it's smack dab against the cliff so I can lean back. Now if it just had a cup holder with a beer in it…"

"I wonder if it's more than luck," Dick interrupted. "Maybe someone rolled it to this spot. It's not only round, but unlike the rest of the base of the cliffs there's no driftwood piled against it."

Lars looked down from his hard rock seat. "By gosh, Dick, you're right. Seems like a lot of trouble to go to for a place to sit."

"Not to sit on but to hide something. Can you help me push and see if we can move it?"

"Ready to rock and roll," Lars replied as he jumped up from the boulder.

Both Dick and Lars stooped down, placed their hands on one side of the boulder and pushed hard. The rock slowly rolled across the sand. "What the heck!" Lars exclaimed as they both looked at the entrance to a cave.

CHAPTER TWENTY THREE

"Sort of like the *Goonies* when they found a pirate ship with treasure inside a cave," Lars said, as he and Dick peered into the opening in the base of the cliff revealed when they'd rolled away the boulder.

"The only kind of ship we'd find in here is one that fits in a bottle," Dick answered.

Lars plucked a small flashlight from one of his vest pockets, "Here, you take this flashlight." He turned it on and gave it to Dick who pointed its beam into the cave.

"The good news is that it gets higher, so once we get through the entrance we should be able to stand up," Dick said.

"What's the bad news?"

"It bends to the left a few feet in, so there's no way to know what's around the corner. How much time do you think we have before the tide starts coming in?" Dick asked tapping his wristwatch. He hoped its water resistance wouldn't be put to the test.

Lars looked at his watch, which was larger than Dick's and had several dials. "We have about twenty minutes."

"No time to waste, then." Dick put the butt end of the flashlight in his mouth so that its beam illuminated the tunnel, got on his knees and crawled through the opening with Lars behind him. As Dick predicted, once they got past the entrance they were able to stand up. Dick removed the flashlight from his mouth and they continued a few more feet until they reached the bend. Dick reached out with the flashlight first and then poked his head around the corner and motioned for Lars to follow him. With Lars glued to his back Dick stepped around the corner. They were in a cavernous room with a sandy floor strewn with boulders. Dick played the beam of the flashlight around the space.

"I don't see any treasure," Lars whispered into Dick's right ear as if someone could overhear them.

"I don't think it would be sitting here in plain sight," Dick replied. "And you don't need to whisper."

"Maybe it's under one of these boulders?" Lars asked, then scurried around giving each of the large stones on the cave floor a hard shove. "They're really heavy and sunk deep in the sand," he said when he was finished. "You'd need a whole pirate crew to move any of these."

"Look, there's another level," Dick said pointing the beam of the flashlight up along one wall. "It's like a balcony."

"And those rocks against the wall below it are like a staircase," Lars added.

Dick swept the rocks with his flashlight. "It does look like someone arranged them into steps."

"Maybe the treasure is up there," Lars said. His excitement reminded Dick of Watson when he was chasing a scent. "Let's go and find out." Lars scrambled up the rock steps without waiting for Dick to reply. Dick followed Lars and when they reached the top, he played his light around the space. "It looks like the shelf is bare," Lars announced with disappointment.

"Let's take a closer look," Dick replied. "Too bad we only have this one flashlight."

"Wait, I can turn on my emergency beacon." Lars said, pulling the ring on his vest. The strobe light popped out and suddenly the entire cave was filled with the flashing light from the emergency beacon. "See, it's like being on a dance floor with the strobe. I heard they're supposed to put you in a trance."

"Let's look around before that strobe scrambles our brains," Dick said.

"Hey," Lars shouted a few minutes later, his voice echoing in the cave. "I think I found something."

Dick walked over to where Lars was standing, his body jerking in the spasmodic light from the strobe. "I think there might be something over here, but it's hard to tell since it's all jerky jerky."

"Turn off your strobe so we can see it standing still with my flashlight."

The strobe light stopped and the beam of the flashlight revealed a pile of rocks resting against the back wall.

"It's just a pile of rocks," Lars said, disappointed.

"Yes it's a pile of rocks, but there are no other rocks around. It looks to me like they were all picked up and stacked against the wall."

"But why at this spot?"

"My guess is there's something hidden behind them."

"Something like treasure." Lars dropped to his knees and began pulling the rocks from the pile. Suddenly he stopped, "I can see a hole in the wall behind the rocks!"

Dick put the end of the flashlight in his mouth again and joined Lars in removing the rocks. A fissure appeared in the base of the wall. After all the rocks were removed, Lars said, "That's big enough to squeeze a treasure chest through."

Dick took the flashlight out of his mouth and pointed its beam into the crevice as Lars looked over his shoulder. "All I see is an empty space," Lars sighed into Dick's ear. "What do we do now?"

"We pile the rocks back to hide the opening then leave the cave and push the boulder back over the entrance. The tide will erase our footprints so no one will know we've been here."

"Why go to all that trouble if there's no hidden treasure?"

"Because Bridgette and Goudy went to all of that trouble," Dick replied as he started placing rocks in front of the opening. "And they wouldn't have unless they had a good reason."

"What's the reason?"

"If I knew that we wouldn't be here. What we've found are clues, Lars, not the solution to the mystery of what Bridgette and Goudy are up to."

"Got it, I guess," Lars said, as he helped Dick cover the opening.

"How much more time do we have before the tide comes in?" Dick asked after they finished and stood up.

Lars looked at his watch then blurted, "It should be starting about now."

"Then we better get out of here."

They descended the stone steps as quickly as they could. When they got to the sandy floor it was still dry, but when they emerged from the cave the incoming tide filled half of the cove. Quickly, they rolled the boulder back in front of the cave entrance. By the time they had finished water was lapping at their feet.

"Looks like we're going to get a little wet," Lars announced the obvious with a chuckle.

"Of course you're laughing. You have a life vest with that emergency beacon and a phone to call the Coast Guard. I've got nothing unless that life vest of yours can keep both of us afloat."

"You mean you want to hold onto me, like hugging?"

"I'm asking you to share your life vest, not give me the kiss of life."

"I never liked the mouth to mouth stuff when I took CPR, even when we practiced on dummies," Lars answered. "Look, I'll wade over to the rocks where the path starts and then you follow, and when you get there I'll grab you and help you up. Without waiting Lars was wading through the tidal surf to the rocks. After climbing up on them he turned to Dick and said, "Okay your turn."

Dick began wading through the water that now came up to his hips as tidal waves broke over him. He stopped, paralyzed, and yelled, "I can't make it!"

"If you stay there the water is going to get higher and with all the waves it'll be like you're trying to swim inside a washing machine."

The good news is I'll be squeaky clean when they find my body, Dick thought as another wave almost knocked him off his feet. Suddenly, he heard a dog barking and through the spray he spotted Watson standing next to Lars.

"Hey, look at that, Watson got loose," Lars shouted.

"He must have known I was in trouble and come to help," Dick yelled back.

"They don't call dogs man's best friend for nothing."

"Best friend or not, Watson's not exactly a rescue swimmer." Just then, Watson bent his head and picked up his leash with his teeth and looked at Dick, then Lars, then back again. "That's it, the leash!" Dick yelled.

"You want me to take the leash so Watson won't jump in the water?" Lars asked.

"No, Watson wants you to throw the end of the leash to me."

"Why?"

"Just do it!" Dick yelled. "Pretend I'm a man overboard and you're throwing me a line."

"Oh, I get it," Lars said with a big grin then took the end of the leash from Watson's mouth, swung it over his head several times like he was a cowboy with a lariat and let it fly.

It sailed through the air and Dick was able to catch it just before it would have hit the water. He wrapped the handle of the leash around his right wrist and yelled to Lars, "Now you pull on it while I wade through the water."

"Okay," Lars hollered and started pulling as Watson barked encouragement.

After struggling through the surging tide Dick got near enough that he could grab Lars' outstretched hand.

"Good thing you didn't tie Watson up that well," Lars said after pulling Dick up on the rocks.

Sitting on the rocks, sopping wet, Dick gave Watson a hug, "Oh, I tied him up really well, but fortunately for me Watson's a real escape artist, a Houdini hound."

CHAPTER TWENTY FOUR

Dora was seated behind her desk, trying unsuccessfully not to fret about Dick falling off the Fishing Rocks and being carried out to sea. Sure, Watson was with him, but what could he do? If he'd only gone along with Dora when it came to choosing a dog for a pet, he would have a Labrador who could dive in and rescue him instead of a bloodhound who would bark and wag his tail. At least Dick had listened to her and taken Lars with him and not relied on Watson to save him if he got into trouble. There was nothing to worry about. Feeling less anxious, Dora was about to return to work on the computer when she was interrupted by Martin who stood in her office doorway and asked if she could meet with Gary Dinger of the Campanology Club.

Dora followed Martin to the parlor where Gary Dinger and Nancy Peale were seated. After exchanging greetings, Dora asked how she could be of help.

"It's not how you can be of help," Gary said. "We would like to repay you for all the help you've already given us in allowing us to practice for the competition."

"We'd like to give a concert for you and all the guests, and anyone else you'd like to invite," Nancy added.

"You mean a private performance?"

"I suppose not entirely private," Nancy replied. "Obviously anyone who is within earshot of the bells will hear it as well," Nancy said.

"That would be most of the town," Martin said.

"I guess it's only fair since they've had to hear us practice as well," Gary laughed.

"I think it's a splendid idea!" Dora said, thinking that it could generate the kind of positive publicity the inn needed to increase its visibility. "We should also do a press release."

"Our club has never done a press release."

"Don't worry," Dora said. "I can write a press release for you … and us. The weather is supposed to be sunny so we can set this up outside. We can also provide the chairs, and Nicole and her partner, Zeke, can provide the catering."

"We need a caterer?" Gary asked.

"We have to provide refreshments, and it can't just be some store bought cookies. We'll cover the cost." Dora's face clouded. "Our current guests check out the day after tomorrow so we need to have the performance before then, if at all possible."

"How about tomorrow afternoon?" Gary suggested with Nancy nodding her head in agreement.

"Perfect," Dora said. "I'll leave you with Martin to work out the details while I get right to work on the press release."

Dora returned to her computer and began tapping out a press release, which was something she had more than a little experience with. In New York, while Dick did his thing, she had worked for a 'boutique' public relations firm. It was a one-man shop, because the owner of King and Associates Communications was a man, Irv King, and all three 'associates' were women. The women called the owner 'Irv the Almighty' and themselves the 'unholy trinity.' Irv came up with the PR 'big ideas' befitting the Almighty, while the trinity had to perform the miracles that made them happen. "Behind every big idea that succeeds are a lot of small ideas that don't fail," was their motto. Compared to those 'big ideas,' the PR success of Bells over Sahalee, as she titled the performance in the press release, would only require a minor miracle.

An hour later, Dora had emailed the press release to all of the media outlets she could find online as far away as Portland and Seattle. Satisfied, she walked back to the front desk just as Dick, Lars, and Watson walked through the front door. Dick was in his bare feet, having left his sodden shoes and socks outside. Dora could tell by his pants that it wasn't only his feet that had gotten soaked. Lars, having shed his waterproof overalls on returning to his truck, seemed to have remained high and dry in his jeans, while Watson had been air-dried while riding in the bed of the pickup.

"Looks like you did some wading in the surf," Dora said to Dick.

"Wading would be an understatement," Dick replied, then recounted their experience.

Dora shook her head when Dick was finished. "You mean after all that, the only thing you found was an empty hole inside a cave?"

"Not just an empty hole, but a hiding place."

"But if there was nothing hidden in it, why did you hide the hole again by covering it with rocks?" Dora asked in consternation.

"Because Bridgette and Goudy wanted it to be kept hidden and we don't want them to suspect that someone knows what they're up to."

"Why on earth do they want to hide an empty hole?"

"I don't know," Dick admitted. "But as Donald Rumsfeld said during the second war in Iraq, we now know what we don't know."

"I sure hope that what we don't know doesn't include that the weapons of mass destruction that were never found in Iraq are hidden in a cave under Cape Disappointment."

"Maybe that wasn't the best quote for our current situation," Dick said. "What I mean is we've narrowed down the possibilities."

"Now it's just a hole full of possibilities instead of a cave full," Dora teased.

"What have you been up to while I was away?" Dick asked, trying to change the subject from his seashore spelunking.

"You can read all about it," Dora said placing the press release on the counter in front of Dick. "Hot off the printer."

After Dick read it he looked up and tapped the sheet of paper. "This concert on the lawn could be a great distraction."

"Really, Dick," Dora replied, pulling the paper out from under his index finger. "It's an attraction not a distraction."

"The best way to distract someone's attention from one thing is to attract them to something else."

"Exactly who are we distracting by attracting them to bells ringing in our steeple and why?"

As Dick tried to think of how to answer Dora's question Cedric Thistlewaite approached them and asked if they were free to hear what they found with their GPR.

"Of course," both Dora and Dick replied in unison.

Once seated in a corner of the empty parlor, Dora asked if they had found a space under the dining room and kitchen?

"Yes," Cedric answered.

"You mean a tunnel?" Dick asked.

"Not a tunnel, more like a basement."

"But we all know that the inn doesn't have a basement," Dora and Dick said in unison.

Cedric spread a sheet of paper on the table in front of them. "This is a rough schematic of the footprint of the kitchen and dining room." Taking a pencil, he quickly drew a rectangle on the schematic. "According to the readings from our GPR what

I just drew is a large space under the kitchen and dining room. It's certainly large enough to be a basement, even though you say there isn't one."

"Could it be a crawl space rather than a basement?"

"A person could crawl in it, but why do that when there's more than enough head room to stand up in?" and with a flourish of the pencil, Cedric wrote in the dimensions of what he had just drawn.

Dora looked at the schematic carefully then shook her head in disbelief. "First we find out there's space between the walls we didn't know about and now we discover there's a space under us big enough to be a basement. Do you think there's an attic we don't know about as well?"

"If there is, it's probably where the skeletons are hidden," Dick replied.

"Did your GPR find an entrance to this basement-like space?" Dora asked Cedric.

"No, but our GPR could have missed a small passageway, especially if it's partly filled in. You could dig a hole in the floor and gain access that way."

"I'm not going to have a hole in the floor of our kitchen or dining room," Dora answered in horror.

"You could also tunnel from the outside under the inn, but it would be more costly and there's the possibility that it could damage the foundation."

"Then we can't do that either. because we can't risk the building collapsing. There must be another way."

Cedric thought a minute and said, "We could bore a small hole and lower a cable with a camera attached. That would give us an idea of what's in the space and it wouldn't be as disruptive."

"I don't know," Dora replied. "This is our busiest season, and it would still disturb guests. Maybe we should wait until winter."

"That's months from now," Cedric said.

"That space isn't going anywhere and if there are ghosts they'll still be here."

"Unless they're snowbird spooks who fly south for the winter," Dick pointed out.

Cedric gave Dick a look that was as withering as the southwest sun and said, "Ghosts aren't geese." Then turned to Dora, "If they're coming from a poltergeist, then they'll get worse. Poltergeists are paranormal bullies, so if you don't deal with them firmly, they take it as a sign of weakness and the next thing you know they'll be smashing dishes and throwing food and ..."

"Sounds like the cafeteria food fights we had in college," Dick interrupted. "We had a lot of people graduate summa cum loud."

Just as a red-faced Cedric was about to hurl a response at Dick, Dora formed a T with her hands and said, "Time out, boys." When they both looked at her, she continued calmly, "Dick and I need to discuss this before we decide what to do."

"Very well," Cedric answered. "But if you want our help you need to let me know no later than tomorrow, because we check out the next day."

"Of course," Dora replied, dropping her hands. "And I want to invite you and your team to a special concert by the Campanology Club followed by refreshments on the lawn tomorrow afternoon."

"There may even be a guest appearance by a supernatural soloist," Dick added.

CHAPTER TWENTY FIVE

"Do you think that we should have Thistlewaite and his gang of ghostbusters drill a hole in our dining room floor to find out what's going on in this space under the inn?" Dora asked Dick after they had settled into a high-top table at the In the Drink Pub. In front of them were two bowls of clam chowder, a cup of tea for Dora, and a pint of Batten the Hatches beer for Dick. It was a late lunch, which is why they were able to get a high-top next to the large window that looked out over the Ilwaco harbor. Boats bobbed in a gentle breeze from the west, as cotton candy clouds floated peacefully in the deep blue sky over the Columbia River and Cape Disappointment.

Dick set down the pint of beer, "Only as a last resort."

"Okay," Dora said, a spoonful of chowder poised halfway between the bowl and her mouth. "What's the first resort?"

Dick smiled, "Use the entrance. It's much easier to walk through a door than a wall."

"How do you know there's an entrance, when Thistlewaite said that their ground penetrating radar didn't show one."

"I think it's more probable that it's a person who is making this racket than a ground penetrating poltergeist, which means that there has to be a way for them to get in and out."

"I don't know, Dick, I think that Captain Johnson would make a perfect poltergeist. After all, he's one of the suspects for the murder of the Reverend and burning down the house where the inn is now."

"Or it could be the Reverend wiggling around for all he's worth," Dick laughed.

"If it is a person making this noise, do you think that they're also responsible for playing the recording of bells in the steeple?"

"I think it's likely the same person or persons. There could be more than one."

"But why?"

"Maybe to create a distraction," Dick shrugged then scooped up some clam chowder with his spoon, deposited it in his mouth, burped, and wiped his lips with a napkin.

"Distraction from what?" Dora carefully sipped a spoonful of clam chowder. Slurping was almost as bad as burping in her book. A book that Dick had never bothered to read.

"If we knew that, we'd know what this is all about and then we'd know who is involved."

"They certainly succeeded in creating a distraction if that was their intent as you suggest. Do you have any idea who this person might be?"

"It has to be someone who has access to the inn."

Dora almost dropped her spoon into the bowl of clam chowder. "But that would mean it's either someone who is staying at the inn ... or one of our employees."

"Exactly, my dear," Dick raised his pint of beer in a toast.

Dora put down her spoon, crossed her arms, and looked at Dick, "And how do you propose that we find this person or persons?"

"Simple. When we find the entrance it will lead us to whoever is using it. Even if we don't catch them red-handed, they're bound to leave clues behind. There's even a good chance that Watson can pick up their scent and we can track them down, or up, since it's beneath the inn."

"That would require a top to bottom search of the inn and the guest rooms are still occupied."

"Not top to bottom, only the bottom since it would have to be on the ground floor."

"That's still four guest rooms on the ground floor."

"If my hunch is right, the entrance isn't in one of the rooms, but in the utility space behind the walls."

Having lost her appetite, Dora picked up her cup of tea and sipped it as she contemplated what Dick said. "When do you propose to do this, and please tell me you aren't going to do it alone."

"Of course I'm not going to do it alone," Dick said. "I'll have Watson with me."

"I think you should take Lars as well. If he hadn't been with you when you explored that cave, you would have been dragged out into the ocean and be halfway to China."

"Or all the way to a beach on Hawaii, but, okay, I'll ask Lars to come along."

She pursed her lips. "If you can't find this entrance, we'll need Thistlewaite's help. What should I tell him?"

"I'm sure you'll think of something, dear," Dick said. As he raised another chowder-laden spoon to his lips he saw Sally Gilmore walking up. Putting down the spoon he greeted her.

"Martin said I would find you here," Sally said taking one of the empty seats at the high top. "I wanted to follow up on the two men in black that Alf told us about. I couldn't find them..."

"Oh, we found them," Dora said.

"What?"

"Sorry, something else came up and I forgot to tell you," Dick said.

"Where did you find them?"

"When I got back to the inn, I found out they had checked in."

"They checked out a few hours later," Dora added.

"So, Alf the bartender got it wrong and they weren't here to cause any malicious mischief?"

"They did cause some mischief, but they contended it wasn't malicious," Dick said then filled Sally in on how the two men had gone into the utility space and came out through a closet in one of the guest rooms.

"I imagine that scared the bejesus out of the occupants of the room."

"Norm and Donna Gamble," Dora said. "They're from Seattle and are here for a romantic getaway."

"They had a 'Do Not Disturb' sign on the room door, but not on the inside of the closet," Dick said.

"They didn't want us to call the police," Dora added. "Although Dick disagrees, I think it's plausible that the two men might have been looking for a cat and stumbled into the room by mistake as they claimed. In any case, Norm Gamble seems to have scared them away with his gun."

"Wait, he had a gun?"

"He said he had a permit for it," Dick said quickly. "He told the two guys that he didn't want to see them again and to tell someone named Chuck the same thing."

"Who's Chuck?"

"Someone he once did business with."

"He called him a sore loser," Dora said.

"What kind of business?"

"Gamble didn't say," Dick replied. "The two guys said they were funeral directors and they denied that this guy Chuck sent them."

"I think I'll do a background check on the Gambles. Can you get me the names and addresses for the two men in black and the Gambles?"

"The two men paid in cash. When I checked the register, their names were illegible, Dora said. "But the address they gave was for a Sweet Bye and Bye Funeral Home in Seattle."

"I'll check out the place," Sally said. "But I'm betting that it's a dead end."

"Sorry I didn't tell you right away, but I got distracted," Dick said.

"Distracted, I'll say," Dora said. "Dick almost drowned."

"I guess I should fill you in on that as well," Dick added, with a grim smile.

After he finished, Sally said, "Cape Disappointment is outside my jurisdiction, so I can't help you with what you found, or didn't find, in the cave. However, I can tell you that there's no law against entering a sea cave unless the park has declared it off limits. Of course, the fact that you didn't break the law when you entered the cave doesn't mean it was a safe thing to do, as you found out. Any other distractions that you want to tell me about?"

Dora looked at Dick, then said, "There seems to be a large space, possibly a basement, that we didn't know about under the inn. The Eidolonic Society discovered it."

"Eidolonic Society?"

"They investigate paranormal activity, and they've been investigating whether there are any of those things going on at the inn."

"You brought in ghostbusters?"

"No," Dora laughed nervously. "The previous owner told them it was okay when they made their reservation last year. It's like a field trip."

"In the twilight zone." Dick hummed the opening bars of the theme song from the sixties television series until Dora gave him a cease and desist look.

Stifling a laugh, Sally asked, "And they found this basement space?"

"They used something called ground penetrating radar to discover it after we told them about strange noises under the kitchen and dining room," Dora explained. "I don't think we're breaking any laws, are we?"

"My jurisdiction doesn't include the enforcement of supernatural laws," Sally said. "But if you happen to unearth anything involving the Reverend Wigglesworth murder that Dick here told me about, I'd appreciate you informing me."

"The Reverend was murdered more than a hundred years ago," Dora pointed out.

"There's no statute of limitation for murder in the State of Washington and it's never too late to solve a cold case, which, in this case, would be downright frigid," Sally said with a wink.

"But whoever murdered him would have died a long time ago."

"That means I can skip the 'alive' part of 'wanted dead or alive'."

After the laughter died down, Sally said she had to get back to work. As she rose, Dora pulled on the sleeve of her shirt.

"Before you leave, we're having a concert on our lawn tomorrow afternoon."

"You need the police for crowd control?"

"More like chime control," Dick replied. "It's a bellringing concert by the Ilwaco Campanology Club."

"There will be delicious refreshments by a wonderful new Ilwaco caterer, Cape D'Lite," Dora added.

"In that case, I'll be sure to make it," Sally said. "As police chief, I have to support local businesses, especially if their product is edible."

CHAPTER TWENTY SIX

Leaving the In the Drink Pub, Dick walked over to the lamppost where he had tethered Watson. Watson was chewing on the untied end of his leash, even though Dick had used a more difficult knot than the one Watson had escaped from on the beach in order to help Lars rescue Dick.

Dora told Dick she wanted to stop at the Grist and Grind to meet with Nicole about the catering for the concert the next afternoon. "I think I told you that Nicole is going to continue working there until her and Zeke's catering business can bring in enough to support them. Why don't you have a coffee and sit outside with Watson while I meet with Nicole?"

"A late latte following a late lunch sounds good to me, and they have a pan with water for dogs so Watson will be happy," Dick said, then looked down at Watson who barked and wagged his tail.

While Dora met with Nicole, Dick took a seat in one of the wooden Adirondack chairs on the patio facing the fire pit with Watson slumbering next to him. Since it was summer and too warm for a fire, the pit was filled with flowers in various shades of red. As he sipped his latte Dick gazed out at the harbor. That's when he noticed Tillie, the owner of Ballast Books. She was sitting on the other side of the pit facing him with a cup balanced on the arm of her Adirondack reading a book, the title of which was obscured by the flaming flowers.

She looked up and their eyes met. "Coffee break?" Dick asked.

"Tea break," she answered, then smiled. "Oh, you're Mr. Carlson. I was so engrossed in my book that I didn't notice you when you sat down."

"I would think that when you took a break from your bookstore you'd take a break from books as well."

"Oh, not at all. I really don't have time to read when I'm working. Although I suppose this is work as well as pleasure, since I'm reading the next book for one of the book groups we host. The group meets at five so I have to finish it."

"I suppose hosting book groups is good for business."

"Yes, but I don't want you to think that we do it as a way to sell books. It's a way to build community."

"What's the book you're reading? I can't make out the title through the flowers."

"*The Murder at Cranberry Manor*. I'm reading it for our Cozy Coast Mysteries book group."

"Since I'm pretty sure I won't be reading it, what's the plot?"

After inserting a bookmark Tillie closed the book. "It involves a murder at an old manor house on the peninsula that's surrounded by cranberry bogs."

"A mystery that takes place around here."

"Oh yes, we have quite a few mystery books where this is the setting. Many of them by local writers including this one. Cozy mysteries are very popular. There's always a murder, but usually only one and death is by poison or some other method that isn't gory."

"I'm guessing it's poisoned cranberries in this case."

"You're close, it's in the cranberry juice."

"I suppose the murderer used arsenic since it's tasteless and has no smell?" Dick ventured.

"Not at all," Tillie replied. "That would be too obvious. The poison is toxicoscordion venenosum, which is commonly known as death camas. It's a plant that grows around here."

"You say the writer of the book you're reading is local?"

Tillie held up the front of the book and said, "She's going to be at the book group today."

"Muriel Binsberry, she's the owner of Flotsam and Jetsam," Dick said.

"She and her late husband opened it several years ago. They'd been coming here for years and when they retired a few years ago they moved here from Portland. Her daughter, Bridgette, lives with her and helps out. Muriel started writing cozy mysteries after her husband, Ellsworth, died suddenly after they opened the store."

"I heard about that," Dick said. "He was swept out to sea at Cape Disappointment and drowned."

Tillie nodded. "Quite tragic. It happened on the Fishing Rocks, which are quite treacherous. Muriel was with him when he slipped off the rocks and was pulled out to sea by the riptide. There was nothing she could do. She started writing cozy mysteries after he died. This is the third one she's written and it just came out."

"She's written three books in three years?" Dick said, shaking his head in disbelief.

Tillie chuckled, "It's not like she's a Jane Austen or James Joyce, but they're entertaining and the plots are quite clever. She wrote her first one in just a month. It was called *Murder on the Headland* and the victim is pushed off the top of the cliff next to the lighthouse above the Fishing Rocks."

"But that's where her husband was swept away."

"A gruesome coincidence." Tillie shivered her shoulders and sipped from her cup of tea.

"My wife Dora loves cozy mysteries," Dick said. "Maybe I should buy one of these Binsberry mysteries for her. It should probably be the first one, *Murder on the Headland*. That way, if she likes it, she can read the others in the series."

"It just so happens I have copies of the other two in my bag here," Tillie said. "I brought them along in case I have time to skim them after I finish this one."

"Is it possible to buy the first one from you?"

Tillie rummaged around a canvas handbag resting on the ground next to her and fished out a copy of *Murder on the Headland*. "If you don't mind a used copy, you can have it for ten dollars."

Dick pulled out his wallet, extracted a ten dollar bill then pushed himself up from the Adirondack chair, walked around the fire pit, and exchanged the ten for the book. Dick slipped the paperback into a back pocket just as Dora walked out of the Grist and Grind.

"Tillie and I were just talking about the Cozy Coast Mystery book group that's meeting later this afternoon at the bookstore," Dick said.

"I plan on joining it in the fall when things at the inn are less busy," Dora replied. "I'm glad I ran into you, Tillie, because we want to invite you to a bellringing concert by the Campanology Club on our lawn tomorrow afternoon at three."

"Since you want to join the book group, why don't we invite the members to the concert as well, honey?" Dick suggested.

"That's a wonderful idea, dear. Would you invite them for us, Tillie?"

"And be sure to include Muriel Binsberry in the invitation," Dick added. Turning to Dora he said, "Tillie told me that Binsberry is a mystery writer as well as the owner of Flotsam and Jetsam."

***

"That was very smart of you to ask Tillie to invite Muriel Binsberry to the concert along with the book group," Dora said to Dick as they walked back to the inn. "We might have a chance to see how she interacts with our Mr. Goudy. What kind of mysteries does she write?"

"The cozy kind that you like and I don't," Dick said. "She started writing them after she moved here. This is the first one." Dick pulled the paperback out his back pocket and handed it to Dora. "I bought it from Tillie."

Dora read the title, "*Murder on the Headland.*"

"In which the victim is pushed off the top of the cliff at North Head Lighthouse and ends up in the ocean near the Fishing Rocks."

"Where you saw her daughter and Mr. Goudy lurking," Dora said.

"And where Muriel Binsberry's husband, Ellsworth, was swept away never to be seen again three years ago," Dick said.

Dora opened the book and read, "'Dedicated to my late husband, Ellsworth, who encouraged me to be a writer.' How ironic that he encouraged her to write and her first book is about someone who was murdered at the same spot where he met his own death by accident."

"Yes, it is very ironic." Dick slowly repeated, "Very ironic."

"Are you going to read it?"

"I may be a criminologist, but as you've reminded me on more than one occasion, dear, you're the expert on mystery books, so just cozy up to this one."

CHAPTER TWENTY SEVEN

Everything was set up for 5 p.m. happy hour. Martin was at the bar, Elspeth was holding a tray of hors d'oeuvres, and Dick and Dora were at their stations, Dick with his left elbow on the bar and a gin and tonic in his right hand, and Dora greeting their guests. Terry Tarantella walked over to the bar where Martin asked if she wanted her usual martini.

"I've already been here long enough to have a usual?" Terry laughed.

"Anyone who stays more than two nights is a regular," Dick replied. "And when you return, which we hope you will, Martin will remember your drink, won't you, Martin?"

"Certainly," Martin smiled and tapped his forehead with his right index finger. "Will Natalya have her usual as well?"

"Yes, please," Terry responded, then said to Dick, "Natalya told me that you had asked her for some help with using social media in your marketing?"

"Oh, right, Dora asked her. I understand she was a great help."

"It really changed her attitude. Whenever I ask her for help with Facebook, she just tells me that I shouldn't be wasting my time on it and should use one of the cooler sites. Of course, she doesn't use the word 'cool' but other words that I can't keep up with like 'dope' and 'sick'. How those words can be considered cool is beyond me."

"What the playwright George Bernard Shaw said about Americans and the English being two peoples separated by a common language can also be said about adults and teenagers," Martin said as he handed Terry her martini.

"Quoting Shaw, now that's impressive," Terry said.

"Last year I was in a production of *My Fair Lady* that's based on Shaw's play *Pygmalion* and our director liked to quote him."

"You were in *My Fair Lady*?"

"I'm a member of our local theater group and they needed someone to play Professor Higgins, so I was drafted. Fortunately, the part doesn't require real singing."

"I can see you as Higgins," Terry said, toasting Martin who bowed in return.

"I had no idea you were an actor," Dick said.

"Just an amateur, nothing like the professional actors you saw when you lived in New York," Martin replied.

"Where's Natalya?" Dick asked Terry.

"She's with Trevor," answered Martha Digby, who had walked up to the bar with Gerald. "They seem to have bonded since their experience with the Ouija board."

"We should thank her and Trevor. Without them, we wouldn't have known that we had a Ouija board and it's an antique that's over a hundred years old. We moved it to a safer place." The safer place being with the Eidolonic Society after Cedric asked if he could examine it.

"You know," Terry chuckled. "Natalya said that the Ouija board was supernatural social media."

"You mean it's some sort of Facebook for the dead?" Martha asked.

"Natalya wouldn't be caught dead on Facebook," Terry laughed. "It would be more like YouTube from the tomb."

"It's funny that Natalya said it was like social media because Trevor said it was like he was playing one of his online games only the person he was playing against was dead," Gerald said.

"Wouldn't that make them offline," Dick quipped.

Terry grinned. "I wonder if they're both on their cellphones now. I told Natalya she could use her iPhone while I was at happy hour."

"We told Trevor the same thing," Martha said.

Dick shook his head. "Why would they want to be on their iPhones if they're with each other?"

"Because they're teenagers, therefore they text," Gerald said.

"Reminds me of those old advertisements for the Yellow Pages, only it's 'let your fingers do the texting' instead of walking," Martin said, handing Martha and Gerald their usuals.

"Can I have everyone's attention?" Dora announced as she stood in the center of the parlor. "You are all invited to a very special bellringing concert by the Campanology Club on the lawn tomorrow at 3:00 p.m. Nancy Peale, who most of you have met," Dora turned to Nancy who gave a Queen Elizabeth wave with her right hand, "will be conducting the concert. Refreshments prepared by Cape D'Lite will be served."

"Does that include booze?" Norm Gamble asked.

"Yes, it will be in place of our usual happy hour."

"Then ring-a-ding-ding, include us in," Norm said, squeezing Donna's shoulders with his left arm.

"Well, with that ringing endorsement, we hope everyone will make it," Dora replied.

Norm grabbed the beer Martin had placed on the bar and handed Donna her usual then turned to Dick, "The Station was as good as any restaurant in Seattle, and we've been to plenty, haven't we, honey?" he said to Donna.

"Oh yes," Donna answered, sipping her chardonnay.

"I'm glad you enjoyed your evening out," Dick said.

"Not as much as the rest of our evening in," Norm rolled his eyes as Donna's face turned pink. "Now that's my blushing bride."

***

As soon as the Gambles left the bar to sit down in the love seat under one of the windows, Cedric Thistlewaite and the other members of the Eidolonic Society took their place. Dick noticed that Cedric had ordered a double scotch on the rocks and asked, "Did you finish giving the Ouija board your expert once over?"

Cedric, his face pale and his hand trembling slightly, gulped down half the scotch then replied, "We not only inspected it we tested it."

"You look like you've seen a ghost," Dick said. "So, it must have been a successful test."

"We were running the Ouija board through the usual battery of tests and decided to ask about the space under the inn that we discovered with our ground penetrating radar..." Cedric paused and took another drink, leaving only a couple of ice cubes in the glass, then jiggled the glass at Martin signaling a refill. "We all had our hands on the planchette and suddenly it started to move wildly around the Ouija board, then the lights went out and the temperature dropped twenty degrees."

"Do you think it was the ghost of Captain Johnson?"

"We didn't have a chance to ask, the lights went back on and the temperature rose to normal. However, the evidence would suggest that it was the Captain. I think he was warning us to not enter the space."

"What do you think would happen if you disobeyed him?"

"Angry apparitions aren't to be trifled with. Lord Carnarvon died mysteriously after defying the curse on anyone entering King Tut's tomb."

"I believe he died from an infected mosquito bite," Dick pointed out, recalling a humorous aside about the so-called curse from a fellow criminologist's lecture on the subject of forensic archeology, most of which was about the possible cause of King Tut's demise.

"Good thing we aren't cursed with a lot of mosquitos around here because of the wind," Martin said.

Cedric took another drink of scotch. "In any case, I will be conferring with my colleagues as to the best way to proceed...or not. I'm inclined to agree with your wife that it might be better to hold off until your peak season is over. It would be best if there were no guests at the inn when we attempt to enter the space. We wouldn't want any collateral damage."

After happy hour ended Dick told Dora about his encounter with Cedric Thistlewaite. "I didn't mention our plan to find an entrance."

"You mean, your plan," Dora said. "Now, I heard some disturbing news as well. Elspeth told me that she saw those men in black in front of the Sleepy Salmon Motel. Apparently they didn't leave town after all. Should we tell the Gambles?"

"I'll call Sally Gilmore. Maybe she can talk them into leaving town."

Dick got Sally on his cellphone and told her what Elspeth had seen.

"I can't pick them up since the Gambles aren't pressing charges," Sally replied. "But I'll go over and warn them to stay away from the Gambles and the inn."

An hour later Sally called back. "I spoke with them. They insist that they really are funeral directors in town on a fishing trip. Apparently they did some shopping because they were wearing t-shirts that they bought from Halibut Harry's..."

"Who's Halibut Harry?"

"That's the name of a guy who runs a t-shirt shop at the port. Very colorful -- both Harry and the t-shirts. They also had some cheap fishing rods that they had bought and said they were going out on a fishing boat tomorrow morning but didn't know which one yet."

"You believed them?"

Sally laughed. "No, but there's no law against impersonating tourists."

CHAPTER TWENTY EIGHT

As happy hour at the Sahalee Inn was winding down, Pete Goudy appeared in the almost empty parlor and walked up to the bar where Martin had quickly placed his usual whiskey sour. After Goudy picked up the glass, Dick pulled a napkin off the bar and handed it to him.

Goudy nodded to Dick and wrapped the napkin around the bottom of his glass.

"How was your day?" Dick asked Goudy with a calculated casualness.

"Same as usual."

"Nothing adventurous, huh?"

"I didn't say that," Goudy replied with a sharpness that cut off any further conversation and walked over to a wing chair in the far corner.

Bafflement was something that Dick was loath to admit, but he had allowed those words to escape while sitting in a chair in the empty parlor after happy hour with a gin and tonic in his right hand while petting Watson with his left. Watson looked up at him with sympathy. At least that's how Dick took it, but it was really hard to tell with bloodhounds because they always had a hangdog look that could easily be mistaken for sympathy rather than boredom. "I can see that you're baffled as well, Watson. What has Pete Goudy been up to on his annual visits, and why did he visit the cave at the Fishing Rocks with Bridgette Binsberry, and why conceal the entrance behind a boulder, and what was inside the hidden space Lars and I found?"

And it wasn't just Pete Goudy's behavior that baffled Dick. Who played the recording of the bells on the steeple speakers? What did Elspeth see that made her faint? Then there were the men in black: who sent them and why are they still hanging around? There's also the Ouija board business with Natalya and Trevor. And what about the noises from underneath the kitchen and dining room? Are they coming from this space under the inn that Thistlewaite and his gang of ghostbusters discovered? And, finally, are all these baffling mysteries connected, or is the Sahalee Inn part of some Cape Disappointment Twilight Zone?

"Well," Dick sighed, "we can't just sit here and wait for the mysteries to solve themselves. The only way to get to the bottom is to keep on digging instead of sitting here drinking, and I can start by finding the entrance to this space under the inn. And no, I don't believe it was Captain Johnson using the Quija Board to warn people not to enter. That means I need to enlist Lars since I promised Dora that..."

Dick was cut off by Watson when he jumped up and barked at Lars who was standing in the parlor entrance. "Your wife said you might need my help," Lars said.

"Exactly," Dick answered, rising from his chair. "I need you to help me access the space that Cedric Thistlewaite and his crew found under the inn."

"You mean there's a basement that we don't know about?"

"What we know is there was originally a house on this site that was built and occupied by a Captain Johnson, a rather nasty but wealthy character, who died under mysterious circumstances. After his death it was acquired by a family who were spiritualists. After a séance that apparently conjured up more than they had counted on, they sold the house and property to the townspeople who wanted to build a church. The house was to be used as a manse where their new pastor would live, and the new church would be built on the land next to it. When the house burned down, also mysteriously killing the first pastor, the congregation decided to build the new church on top of the ruins. That means the ruins of the house are under the inn and it's possible that this space was part of that buried house."

Lars scratched his head. "You're saying that the inn has a house under it, not a basement?"

"Who knows, maybe it's the basement of the house."

Lars moved his right hand from scratching his head to scratching his chin. "If this space is part of some house that was buried under the church, which is now this inn, wouldn't any entrance to it be buried as well?"

"Nicole and Zeke heard noises coming from below the kitchen and dining room and that's where this space is. That means whoever made the noise got into the space through some sort of hidden entry point."

"How are we supposed to find it?"

"My guess is that any entrance would have to be from the utility access passageway between the walls that we were in the other day," Dick replied. "If so, it would have to be on the ground floor near the kitchen and dining room. I need your help to find it."

"When do we look for this secret entry?"

"Tonight, when everyone is asleep. We'll have to be as quiet as church mice," Dick said, then looked at Watson and added. "That includes you, Watson. Not a peep or a bark."

"Wait," Lars, said. "Watson is going with us?"

"Of course," Dick's answer was followed by Watson's concurring bark.

***

At 11:30 p.m. Dick and Lars crept down the stairway to the ground floor of the inn. The only illumination was from the headband lights they wore. Dick had also tied a headband light to the dog harness that he had strapped to Watson's back. At the bottom of the stairs, the hallway to the left led to the ground floor guest rooms, and to the right, to the dining room and kitchen. Directly in front of them was the door to a closet where linens and cleaning supplies were kept.

"There's a door inside here that accesses the utility space," Lars whispered to Dick as he opened the door. Stepping inside, their lights illuminated shelves filled with sheets and towels, a vacuum cleaner, brooms, mops, a bucket, and a big canvas hamper for soiled linen. "I've never been in the utility space in this area but the access door should be behind here." He pulled the hamper from the wall exposing a four foot by three foot door. As soon as he opened the door Watson ran through the opening. "Well, I'll be," Lars said. "It's like he's tracking a critter."

"Or it could be a Goudy," Dick replied.

"Mr. Goudy?"

Dick pulled a napkin from his pocket. "Goudy used this napkin when he got his drink at happy hour. He left it on the bar when he returned the empty glass and it fell on the floor. Before I could pick it up Watson started chewing on it. After a tug of war I got it from him and put it in my pocket. Watson would have picked up Goudy's scent from the napkin."

"You think Watson's tracking him? How cool is that," Lars replied, his headband light moving up and down in the darkness as he nodded.

"Either he's after Goudy or a critter like you said. I guess we'll find out when we catch up with Watson. He went to the right after he entered."

"That means he's not going toward the guest rooms since they're to the left. The only thing to the right is the dining room and kitchen."

Dick bent down and stepped through the opening followed by Lars. Inside, the space was high enough so they could both stand up but only wide enough for them to do so single file. "I can't see Watson," Dick whispered.

They crept forward with Lars' head peering over Dick's right shoulder. After progressing ten feet the passage made a sharp left hand turn. "This must be the wall for the dining room." Dick looked around the corner.

Lars' headlamp joined Dick's. "Well, I'll be," he whispered. "There's a big hole in the floor."

"And there's Watson," Dick added. Watson was sitting next to the hole looking as if he'd just dug up a bone.

After Dick petted Watson and whispered what an outstanding detective he was, he looked down into the opening. There was a vertical drop of about eight feet with a ladder leaning against one side of the hole. "This must be the entrance to that hidden space under the inn," Lars replied kneeling beside Dick and Watson.

"And this was covering it," Dick said, poking at a big piece of plywood. "It must have been pulled over the the hole in the floor when no one was down there, and it's painted gray, and I bet it fits flush with the floor."

"You think Goudy dug this?"

"He could have done it little by little. According to Martin, he's been coming here for years and always stays in the same room. That guest room just happens to be on the ground floor and connected to this same passageway."

"But what's so valuable down there that Goudy would dig a tunnel to get to it?"

"Let's go down and ask him," Dick replied. "I'm pretty certain that he's the person who pulled this plywood aside."

After telling Watson to stay behind, Dick and Lars carefully descended the ladder. At the bottom there was a short tunnel that stopped at a stone wall. There was an opening in the wall where the stone had been removed that was large enough for them to slip through. On the other side was a dimly lit room that was filled with old barrels. Standing beside one of the barrels with a Coleman lantern in his right hand was Pete Goudy. Dick stepped into the room followed by Lars, surprising Goudy, who exclaimed, "What the blazes are you two doing here?"

"Last time I looked I owned the inn and everything under it," Dick said as he stood in the room and looked around. "So, the correct question should be what are you doing here?"

"This was the cellar for the house that once stood here," Goudy answered, placing the lantern on one of the barrels next to him.

"Then I'll rephrase my question, what are you doing in my cellar?"

CHAPTER TWENTY NINE

As a criminologist, Dick was always at least once removed from the crime he was investigating, but here he had actually caught the culprit in the act. Maybe that meant he was now a real detective and not just a scientist. He said to Goudy with more than a little satisfaction in his voice, "It seems we have you over a barrel, Mr. Goudy, so you can save your breath and not try to talk your way out of this by telling us that you just happened to stumble into a hole and ended up here like Alice down the rabbit hole."

"Then you tell me why I would be here," Goudy said.

Dick suppressed the urge to flash a 'gotcha' smile. "You're here searching for the treasure that Captain Johnson supposedly hid, right? Furthermore, the reason why you've been coming here every year and staying in the same room was to dig the tunnel and break into the cellar."

Goudy gave a 'the-gig-is-up' nod of his head, "I'd dig at night when everyone was asleep."

"How did you get through the stone wall into the cellar?" Lars asked. "It's pretty thick."

"I blasted it out with some dynamite."

"That would make a lot of noise and somebody would have heard. You would have woken some of our guests up."

"Not if the rooms were empty, because everyone had been woken by ringing bells and were in the parlor."

"So you're the one who played the recording of the bells ringing that we heard through the speakers in the steeple," Lars said.

"No," Dick said. "Mr. Gaudy, here, wouldn't have had time to do that and then sneak back down here to blow the opening in the stone. It was your accomplice, Bridgette Binsberry, who put the record on and created the distraction wasn't it, Gaudy?"

"Yeah, it was Bridgette," Goudy replied.

Feeling that he was on a roll, Dick continued, "And it was also Bridgette who surprised Elspeth when she went in to clean the ground floor guest room, wasn't it?"

"She got disoriented while going back to my room after helping me clear the ruble from the opening and came out in that one by mistake."

"Elspeth might have been surprised, but she wouldn't have fainted if she saw Bridgette," Lars declared.

"She didn't know it was Bridgette, did she?" Dick said to Goudy.

Goudy shook his head. "Bridgette was wearing a white jumpsuit with a hood and an aerator mask to protect her against the dust, so Elspeth wouldn't have recognized her."

"No wonder Elspeth thought she was seeing a ghost," Lars said.

"Can you explain how the sea cave near the Fishing Rocks figures into all of this?" Dick pressed.

"How do you know about the cave?"

"I followed you the other day and you met up with Bridgette. That's how I know she's your accomplice. You went to the Fishing Rocks where you disappeared around the headland. Then later Lars and I went back to the Fishing Rocks and took the same a path around the headland and discovered the small cove with the sea cave."

"There was a boulder blocking the entrance to the cave that we had to roll away," Lars added. "Inside the cave we found a space with some rocks piled in front to hide it, but the space was empty."

"Because that's where the treasure was going to be discovered, right?" Dick said to Goudy.

"But if the treasure is hidden here, how could it be discovered there?" Lars sputtered.

Dick reached out and put his right hand on Lar's shoulder to calm him. "Goudy and Bridgette were going to move it from here to the cave. If they discovered it here, it would belong to the owners of the inn – us. If it was discovered in the sea cave nobody would think it was Captain Johnson's treasure. Instead, it would be a pirate's treasure."

Goudy nodded his head, reluctantly.

"How were you going to explain how you happened to find this pirate treasure hidden in that sea cave?"

"We have a map."

"You mean one of those pirate maps with X marks the spot?" Lars asked.

"I imagine it will be a bit more authentic looking than that," Dick said. "Right, Mr. Goudy?"

Goudy replied, "Muriel Binsberry made a map on old parchment that showed where the treasure was. She was going to say that she found it on the beach."

"I'd say that claiming you found a pirate map in a bottle washed up on the beach would be pretty suspicious."

"The map wouldn't be found in a bottle but a jug that was sealed shut and buried near the beach. Muriel was going to say that she found it while looking for flotsam and jetsam for her shop."

"I never would have suspected Muriel Binsberry being involved in something like this," Lars said scratching his head.

"Not just involved," Goudy replied. "The whole thing was her and her late husband, Ellsworth's, idea."

"So how did you get involved?" Dick asked.

"We were all members of SMT."

"What's SMT?" Lars asked.

"The Shiver Me Timbers Society," Dick answered.

Goudy shook his head, "You know about that as well."

"We found its website. Amazing what you can catch in the World Wide Web. Tell us more about this idea that the Binsberrys came up with."

"We were researching all the pirates of the Pacific Northwest when Ellsworth read about Captain Johnson, and how he had been the pilot for a ship that carried a fortune in gold that wrecked on Sand Island. He was the only survivor and people suspected he wrecked the boat on purpose and stole the gold and hid it somewhere. All of us agreed that didn't make him a pirate, but then Ellsworth came up with the idea that if we could find Johnson's gold, we could tell everyone that a real pirate buried the treasure. We could point to Iron Jim Sallow burying his treasure and then losing the map he drew as an example."

"And who would be more likely to find a pirate's treasure than some members of the Shiver Me Timbers Society," Dick said.

"We weren't going to just keep it for ourselves, we all agreed to donate half of it to SMT."

Dick laughed, "A gang of philanthropic pirates. Now that would probably make a real pirate like this Iron Jim Sallow roll over in his grave or the bottom of the ocean, or wherever his body ended up."

"I don't think he'd mind if it was used to promote piracy."

"Especially if it wasn't really his treasure."

Goudy shrugged, "Anyway, we started digging deeper, so to speak, and found out that after Johnson died people searched his house and property but couldn't find the gold. Then Ellsworth came across a journal in the Washington State Historical Society Archives that was written by a person who had visited Captain Johnson's house while he was alive. According to the writer, Johnson didn't like anyone in his house, but he let him into the kitchen at the back of the house. When Captain Johnson stepped out to get something from the cellar for dinner, Johnson's wife told the man that Johnson kept barrels of pickled herring, sturgeon, and salmon in the cellar but that he wouldn't let anyone enter, not even her, and kept the door padlocked. The writer of the journal said that he thought that if Johnson locked the cellar then there must be something more valuable than pickled fish inside."

"You concluded that what was locked in the cellar was probably the gold that he supposedly stole from the ship that he was piloting when it was wrecked on Sand Island."

Goudy nodded.

"But why wouldn't they have found it when they searched the house for the gold after he died?" Lars asked.

Goudy gave a rare smile, "Our guess was that nobody thought of emptying barrels of pickled fish. The organizers of the church who bought the house to be the home for the minister inventoried its contents and it included the barrels of pickled fish in the cellar, so they must have been left there by Captain Johnson. Fortunately, we learned from the historical accounts of the church that the Reverend Wigglesworth wasn't fond of pickled fish and the church never got around to disposing of the barrels before the house was burned to the ground."

"Unlike the Reverend, when the house burned down the cellar with the pickled fish obviously survived," Dick said.

Goudy nodded. "Although the beams are a bit blackened from the fire the ceiling didn't collapse. The rubble from the house must have covered everything. We were able to find an account of the construction of the church and there was no mention of a cellar even though it was built on this site. It just said the ruins of the house that had been here were covered with several feet of dirt and the church built on top of it."

"And the church is now our inn," Dick added. "You needed to figure out a way to dig an opening into the old cellar to find the treasure, and you also had to come up with a scheme to keep the treasure instead of turning it over to the owner of the inn."

"You could have just talked to the owners of the inn," Lars said. "Maybe they would have agreed to split the treasure with you. Would have been a lot simpler."

"And legal," Dick added.

"That was our first option, but after all of us spent several days at the inn and met the owner at the time, Farley McTavish, he didn't strike us as a sharing sort of guy, and we decided not to take the risk by telling him."

"Yeah, you're right about Farley, he does have that reputation," Lars said. "But what about Mr. Carlson here and his wife?"

"Things were too far along by then to tell you," Goudy said to Dick. "We figured you'd be pretty upset that we dug the tunnel into the cellar without your permission..."

"That's an understatement," Dick muttered.

"And we'd not only lose any share in the gold, but you'd likely press charges against us."

"So, you finished digging and blasting without telling us."

"How did you find the sea cave?" Lars asked.

"Ellsworth chartered a boat and pretended to go fishing off Cape Disappointment, but really we were looking for caves. He located what looked like a small cave that was near the Fishing Rocks but could only be seen from the ocean. Then he and Muriel went to the Fishing Rocks and pretended to fish. While Muriel fished – she's actually pretty good at it – Ellsworth snuck around the headland and found the cave. He went inside and there was a cranny in a wall that was above high tide level. It seemed large enough for the gold we hoped to find, and we could hide it behind a pile of rocks. They rolled the boulder in front of the cave so nobody would see the entrance."

"I take it that Ellsworth's death wasn't from falling off the rocks while fishing," Dick said.

Goudy put his hands on his hips and slowly shook his head. "If I'd been there maybe I could have saved him. Muriel was there and said that he came back and told her about the cave and then said he'd left his camera inside. He'd taken photos of everything and went back to get it even though the tide was coming in. He got carried away by a big wave from the incoming tide when he was leaving the cave. Muriel said that Ellsworth wouldn't have wanted us to jeopardize our plan by telling anyone what really happened, so she came up with the story about him slipping off the rocks while fishing."

"Did you find Johnson's gold?" Lars asked, impatiently.

"You might as well tell us the truth since we've caught you red-handed," Dick said. "As the inn's owner, I can have you and Bridgette arrested for trespassing, vandalism, and malicious mischief, and Muriel for aiding and abetting the crimes you've committed."

Goudy sighed and then slapped the side of the barrel he was standing next to. "It was hidden in this barrel under a false bottom. The barrel was filled with brine and pickled fish. No one thought of emptying the barrel. Now the brine is all dried out and there are only fish bones. After we emptied the barrel we could see that there was a false bottom."

"It's under the false bottom?" Lars asked, unable to hide his excitement.

"Bridgette and I found the gold last night. We took it out and examined it but we didn't have any bags to put it in so we could carry it back to my room. We didn't want to leave it on the floor so we temporarily placed it back inside the barrel. I came back tonight to transfer it into these canvas bags." He gestured to some bags on the floor. "I was planning to haul it to my room. Tomorrow afternoon when everyone is going to be at the bell-ringing concert outside on the lawn, I was going to hand them out the window of my room to Brigette. We would take it to the cave and dump the gold in the hiding place."

"Where you would discover it with your phony pirate map," Dick said. "Well, now that we spoiled your plan, open the barrel so we can see this treasure."

Goudy pulled the lid off and let it fall on the ground. Dick and Lars walked over to the barrel and joined Goudy in looking inside, their heads almost colliding.

"There's nothing in here but a few fish bones," Lars said, his voice echoing inside the barrel.

After pulling their heads out of the barrel, Dick demanded of Goudy, "Where's the gold?"

"You're the detective, you tell me," Goudy said, clearly surprised.

CHAPTER THIRTY

Goudy was caught red-handed, but the hand turned out to be empty. After finding that the barrel was as bare as old Mother Hubbard's cupboard, they went to Goudy's room where a search found nothing but some dust balls under the bed. One minute Goudy was facing years in prison for stealing millions in gold, and the next he was likely to get off with a slap on the wrist for breaking and entering or, in this case, tunneling. There was no point in playing the bad cop with a bad hand so Dick switched to being the good cop and told Goudy that if he and the Binsberrys cooperated he wouldn't press charges. Goudy agreed. After all, without the gold there was nothing to lose.

Goudy called the Binsberrys, waking them out of their slumber, and told them that he had been caught in the act by Dick who was coming over to their apartment to have a sit down with them. By the time that Dick got to the apartment above Flotsam and Jetsam, Muriel had brewed a pot of coffee. She poured a cup for everyone except Bridgette who was sitting cross-legged in the middle of a couch with a scowl on her face and a cup of tea in her hand.

After everyone else had chosen a place to sit, Dick asked, "Who else knew about your plan?"

"Nobody," Bridgette answered sharply.

"Would Ellsworth have told anyone?"

"Dead men tell no tales," Bridgette replied. It sounded as much like a threat as a fact.

That might be true for pirates, but dead men can be blabbermouths at an autopsy, Dick wanted to tell her, but since he was now playing the good cop he asked politely, "What about before his fatal accident? Was there anyone you can think of who he might have talked to about this plan of yours?"

Bridgette returned to a sulky silence while Muriel looked into her coffee cup. Dick wondered if she was wishing there were tea leaves to read instead coffee grounds. Finally, she said, "Ellsworth talked to many people, almost anyone he met. Not about the plan, but about pirates and their buried treasure. After all, he was the person who organized the Shiver Me Timbers Society, and he felt he had to convince people that there actually were pirates plundering in the Pacific Northwest."

"And finding some pirate's buried treasure would do the trick," Dick replied.

"Not any old pirate, because Captain Johnson's gold was in coins and they would have been minted in the nineteenth century not the eighteenth," Muriel said. "Although Spanish doubloons were still around, the coins were most likely to be gold English sovereigns or American gold dollars."

"They were gold Liberty Heads," Goudy said firmly. "I had a chance to examine them before we put them back in the barrel and the ones I looked at were minted in the 1830s and 1840s."

"In other words," Dick said. "The pirate who would have buried them had to have been plying his trade at about the same time as Captain Johnson would have been acquiring his booty. Was this Iron Jim Sallow swashing and buckling then?"

"Although we don't know when he died because he disappeared, from what we do know, Sallow was active before Captain Johnson would have stole the gold."

"That's why we weren't going to claim that the treasure we found was the one Sallow buried and lost," Muriel said. "The map I drew doesn't have a pirate's name on it."

"Of course not, you certainly wouldn't want to make a false claim on a phony map, would you?" Dick asked rhetorically, followed quickly by a real question. "Even if, as you said, Ellsworth never mentioned the plan to anyone, did he ever mention anyone who shared his interest in looking for buried treasure?"

After knitting her eyebrows in thought, Muriel answered, "Ellsworth did say that he had met a man in Seattle who was interested in finding buried treasure and said that the man offered to bankroll a treasure hunt. However, the man wanted half of the treasure so Ellsworth told the man he wasn't interested, and that was the last he heard from the guy."

Dick's eyebrows arched as he asked, "Did he tell you who this man was?"

"Ellsworth didn't tell me his name," Muriel said. "But he did tell me one thing that I thought was strange. He said that the only thing the man knew about buried treasure was the burying part."

***

Dora sat in her bathrobe and slippers at the small table in the two-room suite at the end of the inn's second floor as Dick walked back and forth recounting his exploits. They were staying there temporarily until they found a permanent place to live. It had a small refrigerator, a toaster oven, and a hot plate. She sipped from a cup of the tea she'd made on the hot plate while listening to Dick. Finally, he stopped and poured some tea from the pot, although he would have preferred scotch, while Dora fed back a summary of what he said, "You and Lars found Pete Goudy inside a basement under the inn that we didn't know existed."

"He called it a cellar not a basement, so maybe we should."

"Alright, Goudy said in this cellar he discovered Johnson's gold that was hidden in a barrel of pickled fish."

"Before they canned fish, they salted it in brine and put it in barrels. It doesn't preserve the fish the way canning does so there are only fish bones now."

"And now the gold has vanished. One could say that it's gone the way of all fish flesh," Dora said with a bemused smile.

"That's one way of putting it, a very clever way, I might add, my dear. The gold has disappeared although not from decay, but theft."

"And you believe him and what the Binsberrys told you when you confronted them? They could be making the whole thing up and there wasn't any gold in the barrels."

"What would be their motive to confess to breaking and entering in order to steal Captain Johnson's gold if there was no gold?"

"In any case," Dora sighed. "The gold, our gold, is gone and all we have are barrels of pickled fish bones."

"Gone, but not far, because whoever stole it from Goudy and the Binsberrys ..."

"... who stole it from us ..."

"That would make it thrice-stolen if you include Captain Johnson's original theft," Dick said.

"Why do you say that this thrice-stolen treasure - I do like the ring of that - isn't far from here?"

"Because I believe there's a good chance that whoever stole it is still here along with the gold."

"You mean they're hiding here," Dora said with alarm, putting down her cup of tea and grabbing a kitchen knife.

"How do we find these thieves?" Dora waved the knife like a cutlass.

"I think they'll reveal themselves at our bell ringing concert, and could you please put down the knife."

Dora put the knife down. "Then we better have the police here."

"We already invited Sally, but I told her that there may be more than bell ringing."

"Shouldn't you ask her to arrest Goudy and the Binsberrys?"

"I promised them that in return for us not pressing charges, they will help us recover the gold." Dick replied. "After all, if it weren't for them, the treasure would still be in a barrel in a buried cellar that we didn't know existed. Now we know there's a treasure that belongs to us."

"I suppose it's enough punishment that they have nothing to show for their efforts," Dora said as she poured some more tea into their cups. "Now tell me this plan of yours. You make it sound as easy as shooting pickled fish in a barrel."

CHAPTER THIRTY ONE

Everything was set up on the lawn in front of Sahalee Inn. Miraculously, the weather forecast had proved correct and there was only a light breeze pushing a few puffy clouds. Not that it couldn't change in a minute. Rows of folding chairs with a printed program for the performance on each seat were arranged on the front lawn of the inn. A table was set up on the patio next to the front door with bite-sized sandwiches, small bags of potato chips, and assorted freshly baked pastries, along with pitchers of lemonade, a coffee urn, and bottles of red, white, and rosé wines, as well as cans of beer in a tub filled with ice. Standing behind the table were Nicole and Zeke. They were decked out in crisp white chef's coats with "Cape D'Lite Catering" embroidered on the left breast under a picture of the Cape Disappointment Lighthouse.

In addition to the inn's guests, there were others from the town, including Morgan Murray who walked to his seat with a plate filled with sandwiches and cookies in one hand and a can of beer in the other. Dick and Dora had reserved the first three rows for the inn's guests. Donna and Norm Gamble sat in the front row between the three Digbys and the two Tarantellas. Both Natalya and Trevor fidgeted in their seats, occasionally bending forward and shooting glances at each other past the Gambles, communicating their boredom the old-fashioned way using their faces instead of cellphones.

As an honored guest, Farley McTavish, the former owner of the inn, was ushered by Dora to a seat in the front row. Cedric Thistlewaite and his Eidolonic Society colleagues were seated in the second row. They had set up their paranormal detection equipment in the steeple, which they were monitoring on a laptop computer. The remaining seats were occupied by other guests, including an older couple from Portland who had come on a bird-watching expedition. This was the first time they had met any of the other guests since they were out of their room each day at dawn and didn't return until sunset. Binoculars hung from straps around their necks and were instantly deployed when an eagle flew overhead and perched on the top of the steeple where it hungrily eyed the food-laden table.

Seated in the third row was a young couple holding hands who had up until now spent all of their time at the beach or in their room. Next to the lovebirds, the seat reserved for Pete Goudy was empty. Instead, there was Morgan Murray's plate of sandwiches and cookies while he himself sat in the last seat. The row behind was filled with Tillie from Ballast Books and members of the Cozy Coast Mysteries book group. Seated in the very back row were Max and Roscoe wearing black t-shirts that they had bought at Halibut Harry's with a picture of Cape Disappointment lighthouse and the words "Disappointment Awaits" on the front in white letters. The t-shirts were tucked neatly into their black pants and their faces were half hidden behind their wrap around sunglasses as well the shadows of broad-brimmed straw hats they'd purchased from Headland Hats.

Dick stood at the back surveying the guests with Sally Gilmore, who asked him, "You really think one of these people is a thief?"

"More than one and now they're going to try and finish their criminal enterprise."

"Unless it's prevented because the would-be perpetrators notice my presence," Sally said, pointing at her badge.

"I'm a great believer in projection of force, but in this case ..." Dick's words were cut off by Dora who stood in front of the assemblage, her arms open in welcome. "We're so pleased to have everyone here for this very special performance by Ilwaco's Campanology Club. They will be performing on the bells in our steeple ..." Dora twisted her torso and pointed at the top of the Steeple where the eagle was still perched, "up there."

"Is that eagle their mascot," Natalya giggled.

"No, he's just waiting to catch any bats that fly out once the bells begin ringing," Farley said from his seat next to her.

"That should be almost as cool as one of my computer games," Trevor said.

"I'm sorry to disappoint you, but the bats are no longer in the belfry," Dora said. "We had them relocated. Humanely, I might add."

"Not half as disappointed as that eagle will be," Norm said.

"Does that mean he'll come for one of us?" Martha Digby blurted with alarm, clutching her husband, who put his arm around her.

"He's not going after prey that is too big to fly away with," the female half of the birdwatching couple shouted with more than a little authority. "Now a dog is another matter."

Watson, who was at Dick's feet, barked fiercely.

Sally whispered, "She means a small dog, like a toy poodle so Watson doesn't have to worry."

"Watson isn't worried about being carried away by old baldy up there," Dick said, stooping and petting Watson. "You just don't want to commit a federal crime by killing an eagle, do you, Watson?"

"We're especially honored that our guest conductor is Dr. Nancy Peale, Professor of Campanology at the Bradshaw Conservatory of Music in Portland," Dora continued. "And here is Dr. Peale to tell you more about what you are about to hear."

With that Nancy Peale joined Dora. After thanking her she said, "On behalf of the Campanology Club, we are pleased to present this special performance. You've heard us practicing in preparation for the Pacific Northwest Change Ringing Competition in Seattle. Change ringing, by the way, is the proper name for the bell ringing that you will hear. It is ringing bells in a sequential manner, which we call a method. So even though the bells won't ring out a tune you will recognize, there is a method in the madness."

Nancy waited for the expected chuckling to stop then continued, "There are literally thousands of methods, with new ones being composed all the time. The names often include the place they are associated with. Today we are premiering a new method that I have written, called *Sahalee Surprise*. Surprise is the class of changes that the method belongs to, by the way, not that there should be any real surprise given all the practice we've put in."

"Not like our first night, huh, when those bells woke us all up," Norm cracked, then took a sip from the can of beer he'd extracted from the tub.

"Oh, yes," Nancy said, without skipping a beat. "It turned out, ironically, to be a recording of a famous method with the name *Cambridge Surprise*. I've probably told you much more than you wanted to know, so now you get to hear our performance. The order of the pieces we will be performing is in the program that you should all have." Nancy looked at her wristwatch. "Now, if you will excuse me, I need to join the ringers in the steeple so the performance can begin in five minutes, at precisely 4:15. The members of the club and I will be available after the performance to answer any questions you may have."

With that Nancy turned and walked quickly to the entrance under the steeple.

Norm and Donna suddenly got up. "Donna forgot her earplugs," Norm announced to those sitting next to them.

"I have very sensitive ears," Donna added.

"Five minutes is plenty of time to just run to our room and get them," Norm said.

Norm threw his empty beer can in the plastic container marked for trash rather than recycling, as he and Donna walked quickly to the front entrance to the inn. Max and Roscoe both got out of their seats and, looking at Dick and Sally, Max said, "We have to see a man about a dog." Watson barked and Roscoe added, "Not a dog dog. We just need to hit the head, the gents' room, in the inn." They walked quickly toward the inn's front door just as Norm and Donna closed it behind them.

Dick whispered to Sally, "I think the game's afoot."

"Look the eagle is leaving," Trevor shouted from the front row. Everyone looked up as the eagle rose majestically into the sky. A minute later the bells began ringing just as Dick and Sally entered the inn.

CHAPTER THIRTY TWO

No one was at the front desk or in the parlor. "I can hear voices from the dining room," Dick whispered into Sally's ear so she could hear over the ringing bells. They crept to the entrance to the dining room and peeked in. Norm and Donna were standing with two huge suitcases on rollers, one black and one pink. Pete Goudy and the Binsberrys stood between them and the door to the rear parking area of the inn where their car was. They could also see Max and Roscoe hiding behind one of the dining room tables where they had crawled on their hands and knees.

"Checking out early?" Pete asked Donna and Norm.

"We decided to beat the rush. Besides, those bells are ruining the romance we've got going, right, Babe?" Norm said, nudging Donna.

"Judging from the size of those suitcases you've packed for a cruise around the world rather than a long weekend in Ilwaco," Brigette said.

Flustered, Donna answered, "I didn't know what to pack so I just brought everything."

"Mind if you show us?" Muriel asked. "Bridgette could use some fashion tips."

"I do not!" Bridgette snapped in response.

"We really need to hit the road," Norm answered, taking the handle of the black suitcase, then said to Pete, "Now if you could just get out of the doorway, we'll be on our way."

"Let me help you," Bridgette said, grabbing the handle of the pink suitcase. "Wow, this is really heavy."

"I packed a lot of shoes," Donna replied.

"I think you've got something other than shoes in your suitcases," Muriel said. "Something that belongs to us."

"What do we have that you would want?" Norm answered.

"Something from a barrel in the cellar right under us," Pete said.

"Yeah, well, I've got something with bullets in its barrel," Norm snarled, pulling a pistol from his waistband where he had hidden it under his untucked polo shirt. "And nobody will even hear the gunshots over all that racket from the ringing bells. Now get out of the way."

"Not so fast," Max said, as he stood up from behind the table with a pistol in his hand.

"Looks like a stand-off," Sally whispered directly into Dick's ear so she could be heard over the sound of the bells.

"You should call for back up," Dick replied.

"I am the back up."

"Let us have those bags or we'll shoot," Max snarled.

"Then we have a problem, because I'll shoot if you try and take them," Norm answered, pointing his gun at Max and Roscoe.

"We're only here to collect what belongs to our boss. We don't want to hurt anyone."

"Haven't you heard of 'finders keepers'?"

"I can hardly hear anything over those damn bells," Max said, then quickly added, "You wouldn't have found it if our boss hadn't told you where to look. He brought you in as a partner and you wanted all of it."

"Some partnership. Your boss gets ninety percent while I do all the work."

"You stole it from us," Muriel shouted at Norm.

"And now you two characters want to steal it from them," Bridgette said to Max and Roscoe.

"And all of you are stealing it from us," Dick announced loudly as he and Sally stepped into the dining room.

"Drop your guns," Sally said, her pistol in her right hand.

"What the hell..." Norm shouted. "It's the innkeeper and the policewoman."

"She's also the police chief," Roscoe said.

"In any case she can't shoot both of us," Max assured Norm.

"Maybe not, but I can get at least one of you. Do you really want to find out which one," Sally said with what Dick thought was remarkable calmness.

"What if I shoot one of these three unless you drop your gun," Norm said, nodding his head at the Binsberrys and Goudy.

"And I'll shoot one of the others. I don't think you want that do you, Chief Gilmore?" Max said displaying a wicked smile.

"Who gets the treasure?" Roscoe asked.

"We'll both take a suitcase," Norm replied. "A fifty-fifty split."

"Okay," Max said. "Take the black one, Roscoe. No way am I going to be seen with a pink suitcase."

As Roscoe walked over to the black suitcase, Dick leaned down and said something to Watson. Watson immediately took off, leapt through the air and sunk his teeth into Max's right hand. Max dropped his pistol, which skittered across the floor toward Dick, who quickly grabbed it and pointed it at Norm. With two guns on him, Sally said to Norm, "Now it's two to one..."

"Don't forget Watson," Dick added as Watson, who had released Max's hand, was now looking at Norm and baring his teeth.

Sally grinned. "That means the odds against you are pretty overwhelming, so lower your gun, put it on the floor and kick it over here." Norm hesitated, but when Watson growled he quickly complied. Watson went over to where Norm had placed his pistol on the floor and picked it up like it was a stick then delivered it to Dick.

"I only have one pair of handcuffs," Sally whispered to Dick after he handed her Norm's gun. "It's not like I have much call to use them."

"I'll get some plastic zip ties from the closet over there that we use for the garbage bags."

"Garbage ties will be perfect for this crew," Sally shot back.

"Take a seat at that dining room table over there," Sally ordered Donna, Norm, Max, and Roscoe. "And put your hands behind your backs."

"And enjoy the bell ringing concert while we tie things up," Dick added, holding up the zip ties he'd retrieved.

CHAPTER THIRTY THREE

Perp walks don't get much more picturesque than the one that took place in front of the Sahalee Inn as Sally and two deputies from the sheriff's department, whom she'd called for assistance, led Donna and Norm Gamble and Max and Roscoe to the waiting police cruisers. All of which upstaged the Ilwaco Campanology Club who had appeared for their post-performance bow before an audience who were gaping at the handcuffed procession instead.

Trevor had broken the stunned silence by shouting, "They caught the bad guys!"

Natalya had followed with, "How cool!"

"Bravo," Morgan Murray bellowed. "A bust accompanied by bells."

"You caught them!" Dora said, rushing over to hug Dick who had emerged from the inn with Pete Goudy and Muriel and Bridgette Binsberry. After a bark, she stooped to pet Watson.

"More like they caught themselves," Dick said than quickly recounted the details of what happened to Dora.

"They had guns?" Dora said with alarm.

"Yes, but we had Watson," Dick replied, then knelt and gave Watson a hug.

"Anyway, the important thing is you're both safe." Dora nodded her head toward Pete Goudy and the Binsberrys who were standing near the inn's entrance. "Did they help like they promised in return for us not pressing charges?"

"They played their part by preventing the Gambles from sneaking out with the gold hidden inside their suitcases."

"Where's the treasure now?"

"It's still in the Gambles' suitcases in the dining room. Since it is now a crime scene the police will be taking the suitcases and their contents as evidence. I asked Martin and Lars to stand outside the dining room entrance to make sure no one entered."

Suddenly the bells in the steeple began ringing. "An encore," Dora said to Nancy Peale.

"Not by us, as you can see the entire Campanology Club is here." She gestured to the members of the Ilwaco Campanology Club who were eating post-performance pastries from Nicole and Zeke's refreshment table.

"Then some prankster must have snuck in," Dick said.

"A prankster who knows change ringing because that's a method called *Plain Hunt*," Nancy said.

"And it takes more than one person on the ropes to play that," Gary Dinger added, a half-eaten piece of cranberry strudel in his right hand.

"We're seeing some unusual activity on the monitoring instruments we set up in the steeple," Cedric Thistlewaite interrupted, holding up the screen of his laptop.

Dora and Dick looked at the screen while Cedric explained what the lines on the graphs meant. "The data indicate possible paranormal activity after the Campanology Club ended their performance."

"It's not a recording, because we've removed the speakers from the belfry," Dick said.

Suddenly, Watson barked and ran toward the open front door of the inn. "Now what's gotten into Watson?" Dora said.

"He's picked up something," Dick answered. "We better find out what."

Leaving Thistlewaite staring at the screen of his laptop computer, Dick and Dora ran to the front door of the inn where they met Sally who was walking back from the police cruisers with another police officer.

"What's going on?" Sally asked. "We're just headed back to the dining room to go over the crime scene and impound the suitcases with the gold as evidence."

"No idea," Dick replied. "The bells started ringing seemingly by themselves and then Cedric Thistlewaite told us something paranormal might have happened in the steeple and then Watson took off for the inn's front door."

All four of them followed Watson's barking to the entrance to the dining room. Martin and Lars were standing in front of the doors as Watson barked, frantically wagged his tail, and sniffed at the closed door. "What's gotten into Watson?" Martin asked.

"Something inside the dining room doesn't smell right to him is all I can say," Dick replied.

"We locked the door just as you told us, Chief Gilmore, and we've both been standing outside," Martin said.

"Nothing has gone in or out of there," Lars added, his right hand wielding a wrench.

"Whatever it is, we need to get in there and examine the scene of the crime, so unlock the door," Sally said.

Martin inserted his master key into the keyhole, turned it and pushed open the door. Immediately, Watson shot through the open doorway. He stopped several feet from the suitcases and started barking again.

Dick went over and commanded Watson to stop barking. "He seems to be disturbed by the suitcases, although they're just where we left them."

"Then he'll be happy when we get them out of here and to the police station where we can inventory what's inside," Sally said.

"Since there's a lot of gold in them they'll be pretty heavy," Dick said. "You might want to bring a police car around back and we can take them out the rear exit."

"Good idea," Sally agreed and ordered the police officer standing beside her to get the cruiser.

Suddenly, Watson scampered over to one of the suitcases and pushed it with his nose. It began to roll across the floor."

"That's strange, that Watson doesn't seem to have a problem moving it," Dick said, running over and grabbing the suitcase handle to stop it. "I'm not discounting the push power of Watson's nose, but a suitcase full of gold shouldn't move that easily." He lifted it by the handle. "It feels empty."

Sally pulled on the handle of the other suitcase. "Same with this one."

"We better open them here rather than the police station." Dick pulled on the clasp. "This one is locked."

"It should be, since I locked both of them when I finished checking their contents after arresting the Gambles, Max and Roscoe. Both of the suitcases were filled with bags of gold coins," Sally said. She took the keys from her pocket, knelt down and unlocked one of the suitcases and opened it.

"It's empty!" Dora exclaimed, holding her hands to her mouth in astonishment. Sally tossed a key to Dick who unlocked the other one. He stood and scratched his head in consternation, "This one is empty as well."

"Like I said, the bags of gold were in them, since we opened them with these keys that the Gambles had used to lock them." After a quick examination of both suitcases, Sally said, "The locks to the suitcases haven't been jimmied and I have the keys."

"Could the Gambles have an accomplice who also has a set of keys to the suitcases?" Dora suggested.

Sally nodded her head, "They could have snuck in and taken the treasure."

"I swear that we didn't let anyone inside the dining room," Lars blurted.

"And the only key to the dining room other than this master is locked inside the key cabinet in the office," Martin added.

"What about the rear exit door?" Sally asked, pointing at a door with the red exit sign over it.

"It can only be opened from the inside," Martin said, walking over to the door and pushing on a lever to demonstrate.

"And I just now checked all of the windows and they're locked and the glass isn't broken," Lars said.

"How could all that gold disappear if the suitcases and the room were locked, we have the keys, and there's no sign of any forced entry?" Sally asked, shaking her head in disbelief.

"I don't think that even an escape artist like Harry Houdini could pull something like this off," Dick admitted, reluctantly.

CHAPTER THIRTY FOUR

Dora and Dick sat on the loveseat in the parlor of Sahalee Inn with Watson snoozing at their feet. All of the guests had left and the new ones had not checked in. Martin had mixed them both Long Beach iced teas. Dick raised his glass in a toast, "Here's to the arrest of the Gambles and the men in black for attempting to steal Captain Johnson's treasure and resisting arrest."

"Resisting with deadly weapons," Dora clinked Dick's glass. "And what about this Chuck fellow, who hired the two men in black, will he be charged with anything?"

"Max and Roscoe implicated him so Chuck will be charged as well. He's a kingpin in the Seattle underworld."

"How appropriate for someone whose front is an undertaker," Dora said before taking a sip from her glass.

"Unfortunately, we are still left with the mysterious disappearance of the treasure," Dick sighed. "We've searched the inn thoroughly, including the guest rooms and our guests' luggage before they checked out and didn't turn up even a trace of it. It's as if it vanished into thin air."

"If it's the ghost of Captain Johnson, I'm sure he found a better hiding place this time than a barrel of pickled fish," Dora said. "In a way I'm glad that he reclaimed his treasure since it means his ghost won't be ringing bells and engaging in other frightful things that disturb us and our guests."

"I think there's a more probable explanation for the disappearance of the treasure than the ghost of Captain Johnson."

"What probable explanation?" Dora said, nudging Dick with her left elbow. "Have you forgotten what your favorite detective, Sherlock Holmes, said about improbable explanations being true after you've eliminated the impossible ones?"

"No, but to quote my newly favorite detective, Hercules Poiret, I'm working on it using my little grey cells," Dick said tapping his forehead with the tip of his right forefinger. "And when I find out what the explanation is then there's a good chance I can find the treasure and even more importantly, solve the murder of Reverend Wigglesworth."

"I knew you would be more interested in solving a murder than finding a fortune in gold," Dora laughed, playfully jabbing Dick in the ribs with her elbow. "At least if you're right you'll prove that if we do have a ghost he's not a murderer."

"He could be she," Dick replied.

"Whatever it's ghostly gender, just remember that while you're working on these mysteries, we still have an inn to run."

"I haven't forgotten."

"No, but your first love is solving mysteries."

"My second love, my dear. You are my first." Dick put his left arm around Dora. As they leaned toward each other to kiss, Watson suddenly woke up and barked.

"What is it now, Watson," Dora asked. "A ghost, a crook, a bat, or a critter?"

Watson barked again and then ran out of the parlor. Instead of getting up and following Watson, Dick laughed, "Whatever game's afoot, it can wait."

THE END

ACKNOWLEDGEMENTS

I want to acknowledge the following:

My friends Leanna and Kevin Moos whose experience as the owners of the Inn at Harbour Village in Ilwaco provided the impetus for this book.

My copy editor, Elizabeth Baer, for her excellent work at transforming my often wayward grammar and spelling into a readable book.

Ilwaco artist Don Nisbett for the wonderful book cover he painted.

And, finally, my wife Kathleen Sutcliffe who read numerous drafts, made wise suggestions and encouraged me to "get it done".

ABOUT THE AUTHOR

T.P. Wintermute writes novels, short stories and essays and is also the publisher of the Prismatist eMagazine (www.prismati st.com). He spends part of the year on Cape Disappointment in the southwest corner of Washington State, which is the setting for this book. Prior to being a full-time author and publisher he was the executive director of a charitable foundation in Detroit, Michigan.